Heartbreaks & Homeruns
Mika C.C.

Falling For The Angels Book 3.

Cover designed & created by Mika's Husband.

Edited by Amanda.

Trigger Warnings: Mention of miscarriage and loss of a farm animal. Body shaming and self shaming. Mention of fatphobia and bullying. Talk of PPD, depression and trauma.

To my daughter,
in hopes she'll find a husband who loves her and all of her, all of the
time.

This story is also dedicated to
every plus-size woman who's ever felt uncomfortable in their skin,
there will always be someone out there that loves you.

Contents

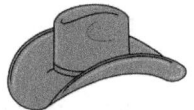

Prologue

RICHARD - 3 MONTHS BEFORE

"Did you watch the game tonight?" I ask as I walk into the kitchen and see my wife washing dishes that she doesn't need to do, not when our maid could've done it. I imagine Amelia must've dismissed her earlier and that this is just a way for her to feel as a housewife.

"I did." Amelia said with a slight smile.

"So you saw the catch, then? I'm surprised my arm didn't get pulled out of its socket, reaching for the ball. I'm surprised Hayes didn't try to run for it when it seemed to almost reach him."

"Your arm must be sore then." She rolled her eyes as she turned away, focusing back on the dishes she was rinsing.

"A bit, but nothing my masseuse can't fix." I respond with a smirk, hoping she'd look up and get the hint, "You know I was thinking—"

"A man hit on me tonight."

My eyes go wide. "What?"

"A man. He hit on me tonight when I was out, watching the game with Lily."

"A man *hit on* you. And you told him you were married?" The initial shock begins to wear off, as I know and trust my wife.

"No." Amelia says, stopping the faucet from running, "I didn't feel like it."

I feel my heartbeat pace with anger building as she continues to speak.

"It was the first time I felt appreciated and wanted—the first time in a long while that I was seen as someone other than Ramsey Greene's wife. And I liked it."

"Amelia." I try to say her name as softly as I can without the fumes of anger coming through my tone of voice.

"It's been years since I've found a voice to listen to, but tonight was confirmation."

"What do you mean, *confirmation*? Of what?"

"I'm tired of being someone I'm not, Rich. I hate that I have to tell you this way, but I'm done."

"*Done?*" I ask as I watch her slip her wedding ring off her finger. I'm even more confused as I watch the sparkle of the ring settle on the kitchen counter.

"I can't do this anymore. And I can't be the only one to put the work into this marriage anymore."

"Amelia, stop." Feelings of anger and confusion cloud my vision, but it's always been Amelia to clear my darkest feelings.

"I've seen the way you are when you play; I've seen the way you are with your fans. Even some of your teammates I've seen you laugh with."

"I can *promise* you, no teammate has made me laugh."

"Maybe it hasn't been, but I've seen you smile around them; I've seen the way your face has lit up at that *cafe*." Through her voice, I can hear it. I can hear the way she feels about me having a female friend.

I don't, not really. I've only talked to her a handful of times, but it's obvious my wife is feeling jealous and perhaps a little possessive over me lately.

"Amelia." I try to say with a tone that will let her know that she has nothing to worry about.

"No. You don't get to use that tone." Taken aback by her bite, I try to explain.

"You don't even—" She speaks up, interrupting my sentence, something she's never done in the past.

"Yes, I do. I know that tone means you think I'm being unreasonable, that you think I'm making it all up. That I'm insecure." I watch her throat bob as her voice wavers, "There's no insecurity when I see that you are much happier with everyone else but me. Your calling has always been behind a bat or baseball glove, so I get that. I don't want to take it away from you, so you can keep it."

"Ames." I grabbed her hands, not even worried about the ring she put on the counter.

"I'm making it easy for you. I'm letting you live out your dream, so you can be who you are."

"That's not making it easy for me." I say with a deep sigh.

"Please. This is the easiest and best thing for you. So take it while you still can." Amelia says before ripping her hands out of my grasp and heading towards the door. I follow on her heels, watching as she pulls a bag out of the linen closet. Ames looks back at me, jumping a little as she's startled that I followed her. Have I been so blind that I didn't notice her bag when I'd hung up my hat? Have I been that distant that she didn't expect me to follow? Either way, my wife takes one look at me and lets out a small sigh that sounds like she's a thousand miles away instead of a few feet in front of me.

"I'll have Lily pick up the rest of my things later this week." Amelia says as she opens the front door.

"Ames, we can work this out. We can go to marriage counseling; I can try harder. I can—"

"You can, what?" She turns to look at me with her head cocked to the side slightly. "Retire? Is that really what you want? You have to know that it's not going to be enough. I'm never going to be enough for you if you were to give it up."

"Amelia, that's not—"

"Stop trying to deny what I know is true. I know you, Richard. I've known you since we were sixteen, just as you've known me. Does this look like the face of someone who wants to give up?"

"Amelia, I don't want you to give up."

"I know you don't, but I can't stay here a minute longer feeling like I deserve more. I deserve better, Rich. And—" I hear the beep of a car as both me and my wife look out to the dark car with its lights on, waiting for her. "I can't do this anymore. Don't follow me, please." With that, Amelia presses a light kiss to my cheek before she and her bag nearly sprint to the cab. I watch from the door as her driver puts away her luggage and Amelia slides into the backseat. Both doors close at the same time, as I'm left to look at the marks of the tires on the driveway.

Amelia - 2 months before

My friend Lily's apartment was a complete wreck; I had totally forgotten that she was a single mom and had only offered her place as a nicety. I felt bad the entire time I spent sleeping on her pull-out bed, especially when her daughter would wake up crying and I never knew what to do. I had never been around kids, and being around Lily and her baby had taught me a lot. Even just watching a mother bond with their child made me break. I had wanted a baby for so long, and it never stuck. Richard and I had tried, but life got in our way.

Even though I had moved out and planned to leave the state, Richard called and begged for therapy. As much as I fought against the idea of marriage counseling, I caved. We went for a month, as the therapist made our problems her problems. Talking it out was my biggest issue; I couldn't. I couldn't talk it out with Richard just the two of us; how either of us thought counseling would help was the biggest waste of money. There was so much history between Richard and me. The heartache and infertility were something we both knew about; we knew it wasn't going to happen, not without intravenous measures. We never spoke about it after the gynecologist delivered the news.

In the last year of our marriage, we hardly looked at each other, rarely ate in the same room, and rarely had time to sit and talk about our days. Richard was always on the clock with baseball; even his off-season workout regimen took him away from me. Our sex life had still been active, but it wasn't the same...

"Fuck me." I begged. Perhaps I should've waited until Richard had driven me back to Lily's apartment complex, but I didn't care where or how; I just needed to know if I had been imagining it or if making love to him had truly changed.

"Amelia, I'm driving." Richard says with a scoff.

"Pull over." I look over at him as he quickly glances at me.

"You're that serious about me fucking you? Were you even present at that counseling session?"

"Shut up and fuck me, Richard." He risked another glance at me before pulling off to the shoulder of the highway.

"Get in the backseat." Richard demanded, as he broke the buttons off his shirt just to show me his chest. His very muscular, defined chest—a part of him that looked better with age and the more he worked out. I followed his order, my husband close behind as we quickly made it into the backseat. His lips pressing directly into mine as we wrestled our clothes off each other. The moment Richard sees me naked, he sighs, a noise I very rarely heard, but once both of us sat down, him on the leather seat, me wrapped around him, my thighs spread apart to straddle him.

Richard looked up at me. "You're amazing, you know that?"

I hummed as I felt his fingers push my hair back; a quick peck was all we gave each other. I let my body do the rest, letting my pelvis thrust against him, letting Richard hump and touch me until both of us were ready. His hard cock always took a minute to enter me; this time was no different. I rode his cock until he switched our position around, and he fucked me with him on top. Nerves got to me with my weight gain; I worried I didn't look as sexy on bottom, with skin folds and a double chin that lasted for days. I moaned, trying to focus on his dick inside of me instead of how I looked to my husband.

The moment he asked me to turn around was when I knew the results... Richard fucked me harder from behind, with his hands just barely on my hips, but it wasn't enough. I had tried to enjoy his soft touches, but they weren't the same when my husband was obviously afraid to touch my fat. He used to grab me when I was skinny and hold onto me like I was his lifeline. What had changed between then and now shouldn't matter. I groaned; it came out like I was getting close, but he couldn't see my face to even know if it had been real or not. Richard pulled out and didn't even bother to ask for me to turn around. He never bothered to ask for help; it had been like this the last few months. I turned anyway to watch him jerk himself off, watch as he barely looked at me, just solely focusing on his dick as he pumped it tight in his hands. Watching the cum seep into his hands rather than inside of me.

Richard was a beautiful man; he was an amazing lover and an even better person. How he couldn't see me die inside, see the hurt in my eyes over me not being able to make him come. How I barely helped; I wasn't even the focus that made him come. I closed my mouth before I said anything; I couldn't. If he wouldn't bother to look at me, I wouldn't bother to say it. My husband should've known that he should've looked me in the eyes. He should've looked at my breasts or fucked me until he could come inside me. None of it seemed to dawn on him, not when I handed him a tissue, not even when I got dressed. Everything about the sex felt wrong.

Once I separated us, with me in the passenger seat as he dressed in the back, I knew what was to come. I knew he'd ask me to move back home. I knew he'd keep pushing for more counseling sessions. I'd come to the realization that the pattern we'd fallen into wasn't productive; it was insignificant. We'd become the couple that my parents' friends would gossip about to them. I couldn't live with that kind of relationship; I couldn't survive it, let alone *try* for something that wasn't there.

Richard heaved a breath as he pushed through the center console to get back into the driver's side. Neither of us dared to speak or even look at each other—not a compliment or even an explanation. A simple ride in silence, nothing but the sound of the wind from the rolled-down windows. Whatever it was on both of our minds was too loud to speak; the bumpy road to Lily's apartment was the last of our silence as I readied to let myself out.

"Please, let me get your door." Richard said before he got out and ran to the passenger side to open my door. The second the door opened and our eyes locked, my thoughts spilled out.

"I don't want this. I don't want counseling. I don't want the horrible sex. I can't. I have to get out of this place—you have to let me leave. You can't keep me in your bubble. I can't live with this unhappy feeling anymore, Richard." The world seemed to tip on its axis once I finished speaking.

I watched as Richard's jaw flexed. "You're right. I can't stop you from leaving. At one point I did think my bubble was actually our bubble, but you're right about that too."

"I'm sorry—"

"I'll do whatever it takes to make you happy, and that's my problem. So if I have to spend my life without you to make you happy, I'll do it."

I feel my brows crease with his words, "Really?"

Richard nods, "If you need this that badly..."

"Just a few months, no contact. I just can't live in this environment, this feeling right now." I say as I watch his brows do a dance from confusion to understanding.

"A few... Sure." I look at his neck as he swallows the words, and as they hit him harder, I notice the bite of his cheek, but he opens the car door wider. "Will you call me when you're ready to come home?"

I blink as he helps me out of his car; I don't know how to answer his words without lying. I've never lied to my husband, not ever in our lives, "Yes." The fib comes from my lips so freely, just as fast as the regret turns in my stomach. I let Richard kiss me on the lips, as I know it's possibly the last time. The kiss doesn't deepen, it was little more than our usual short pecks, but it certainly didn't linger. When our lips part, I fake a smile, just as he does too.

As if on cue, a low rumble of thunder settles into the earth. Richard growls at it like he can control the weather. The amount of rain in Florida is almost as exhausting as the drought in California. This moment can't last any longer, despite what he may want, and the rolling clouds are the perfect excuse.

"I'm going to go before it starts to rain." Both of us say at the same time. I want to smile at our knack for saying things simultaneously, but I know that's about to change, so I give him a small upturn of my lips.

"Bye." I say first.

"Until I see you again, Turtle." Richard says with a wink. My lips open as I watch him run to the car and get in. I hadn't heard my husband use my nickname in so long; I thought he forgot it or just realized how ridiculous it sounded. I held myself together long enough

MIKA C.C.

to watch Richard drive off and wonder what the hell I'm going to do
with my life without him in it.

Chapter One

Richard - Present

Every day I step onto the baseball field a little more tired than the last. It's been this way for a while now. I had everything I ever wanted—well, almost everything. It's been three months since I've last seen my wife. Three months of her no contact order—not a separation but an order that we shouldn't speak from her very lips. The last time I spoke to her, she begged for space from me. All of it had been surreal, and yet I still remember the day like it was yesterday.

Except it wasn't. I wasn't in my house; my wife wasn't by my side. I was on the field, watching the ball come toward me like I wished Amelia would come back to me. There was so much wrong with my life now, at least personally; career-wise, everything was right. I took shit from no one, talked only when spoken to, and spent most of my days doing what I loved. Baseball had always been what I loved, what I grew up learning, and what I always wanted to do.

I'm always reminding myself of where I started, on a small little field across the country, playing t-ball with my brothers and the kids in the neighborhood. We'd done everything together—at least my parents had forced us to, since four kids outnumbered them. Growing up with siblings should've made me want to be around them more, but the truth was, I wanted more peace. I never had the time to be on my own. I never had the space to know who I was. Now I was almost forty, living in a two-story house by myself and wishing I had that sense of family back.

When I thought of my goals, especially my life at forty, I always thought Amelia and I would have it all. A big family of our own, a home we could grow in, and enough money so we could visit our families whenever we wanted to. I expected it, I planned for it, and I let it all fall apart.

Amelia didn't have to tell me I was a horrible husband; I knew I was. As a professional baseball player, I hardly had any time for my wife. I hardly spent any time at home when half of our games were out of state. Teammates would get married, and it'd be mandatory for me to go. Amelia had always been by my side for weddings, but after spending so much time trying for a family—well, I couldn't blame her for not wanting to see groups of families together with their kids. Not when we had dealt with our own problems with fertility...

Just the thought of Amelia and everything we'd been through—everything we put each other through—was enough to put me in a depressive state. I'm not sure she ever knew it. I had even spoken to the shrink my coach recommended. The shrink was quick to diagnose me and put me on antidepressants, but the second I noticed that it affected my game, my catching arm more specifically, I stopped taking them. Falling back into such a depressive state, I managed to fuck up the one relationship that really mattered.

I should've given myself time. I should've given myself grace after the worst day of my life, but I couldn't let Amelia see me down, not when I saw how she struggled with it herself. Seeing her fall and knowing she blamed herself was the worst part of it all. I couldn't imagine how she felt, no matter how bad it got for us. I'd always been her rock, and if she saw the rock crack, she'd have nothing to hold onto.

"Greene!" I hear a shout to my left and turn to see Capsley eyeing me. I nod in answer as we both look up at the ball teetering between his side and mine. Thankfully, this was just a postseason game, and I could let the ball go to him. I didn't have it in me to bother catching it, not with my wife gone from my life. I could hardly remember what it felt like to love the game. Loving baseball went hand in hand with loving Amelia.

I watched the ball fall from the sky, coming faster and spinning as rapidly as my mind did. No matter how much I didn't care about the game, I still saw the ball as the one thing that kept me from crumbling. I reached out my gloved hand and caught it. I could hear the exasperated sigh from Lane Capsley in the same moment. I looked over at him, the hard stare in his eyes, the way he looked equally angry and concerned. I was unsure of what he knew, but sure that he knew something was wrong.

"What's going on with you?" Lane's voice almost drowned out by the sound of me slamming my locker shut.

"Nothing." I answer, pulling my shirt over my head.

"No. Nah. Don't pull that shit with me, Rams. I know something is wrong with you. You've never played a shitty game in your life.

3

Ever since you missed the game a few months back, I've noticed the difference."

"There's no difference, Lane." I say as quickly as I avert my gaze to something other than his eyes on mine.

"Either you tell me what's going on or I get Coach Guntz involved. And in case you didn't realize, when he's not here, I'm in charge, so if you don't want to get fired—"

"I'm quitting, Capsley." He's known for a while that I've been on the edge of retiring; all of the players have. The entire league has been talking about it for two years now. But that doesn't stop the shock that takes over Lane's face.

"Wait, for real this time?" He scrunches his face, "I mean—you keep saying it; Guntz has even talked about Hayes replacing you, but—"

"It's for real this time. I'm not sure I want to even finish this season."

"Wait, what? You can't just *leave* leave. What about the NLDS?" The stern look on my face should tell him enough, but his expression of confusion doesn't falter.

"I have bigger problems of my own." I say as I watch Lane look around the locker room. It's fairly obvious that he's going to be secretive with his next words.

"Is Amelia–" Capsley then uses his hands to gesture around his stomach, "Because you know, Nova could really use a—"

"No." I snap before he can take his sentence further. "My wife, Amelia, is not pregnant." She can't get pregnant is what I want to say to him, but I hold it in for fear of even letting myself be vulnerable with the guy. Capsley of all people would be the one idiot to knock up

4

our coach's daughter. He was lucky enough to get her to marry him just a few months after she had their baby. I know I should be happy for him, and I was when he told me when she was first pregnant, but the moment it settled into my thoughts was the moment I felt both jealous and depressed that it wasn't me, that it hadn't been Amelia's.

"Oh. Sorry." Lane says softly, "Is everything okay with Amelia? I haven't seen her in—"

"Not since the World Series, I know." I roll my eyes and get my duffel bag prepped for my ride home. I let Lane talk as I looked for my keys.

"Really, that was the last time? No. That can't be. I just saw her at the bookstore with Christian's ex like a few weeks ago." I jolt upright, my body going rigid as Capsley finishes his sentence.

"What? She's back?"

"Back? Back from where?" Lane looks confused with his dark brows furrowing into his nose.

"She visited family for a few weeks..." I lie through my teeth; I've never been great at lying. Amelia's always been quick to know when I had in the past, but Capsley doesn't know me that well.

"Oh. Well then, I guess so? I didn't know she was close with Chelsea like that. You know Chelsea's like back, right? Must be awkward for Chris..."

"I should go," I say, pausing whatever else Lane was going to say next to me.

"Okay. Good talk?"

"Very good." I answer flatly, with a hand on his shoulder. Capsley grins like an idiot.

"So you're staying for the rest of the season?"

"We'll see." The smile I give is fake, barely showing my teeth, but he doesn't seem to notice that my words never hold any water, not when my wife is my priority.

The moment I got home, I looked for her. I looked for Amelia everywhere. If she had been back as Lane had said, she'd have to have come home, at least to sleep. The moment I open her side of the closet tells me I was wrong. Lane had been right about one thing. Amelia was here; she had been in the house, but it was not to sleep. I look around her empty closet, nothing but a single piece of paper taped to the pole with hundreds of plastic hangers on it. I want to rip the paper; I know it says the words I don't want to read. I know her written words are laced with heartbreak and tears. I can feel the heaviness in the air that surrounds this house. I can feel the ghost of her; I can still smell her perfume, like Amelia was here recently. This house was my love letter to my wife, and now I'm left with a broken heart and a bad breakup letter.

Richard,

I'm sorry that I wasn't able to do this in person. I hope this doesn't come as a complete surprise, but I just came back for the rest of my things and had a friend's help. I'm only staying with her for one more day, and then I'll be gone. I'm going back home and couldn't really leave all of my clothes in Florida. I know this isn't what you wanted or expected, but you had to have known this part was coming. As much as I want to tell you the reason I left, I know you know why, somewhere deep down I know you know. I'm glad you've understood my need for space and the no contact order, so as much as I've appreciated it, I've reached out to a lawyer about taking the next steps in our separation. You should be getting some mail in the

---

next few days. I hope it all makes sense. I'll send another update when I'm ready.

   With Love,

   A.

Chapter Two

Amelia – Present

"You live with two other guys?"

"They're on the team," Graves says as he pulls the gear shift into park. "You're the one that came here without a plan."

"I know. I'm fine with it; it's just..."

"Just what?" Graves brows meet as he looks at me with his intense stare.

"You're not... Is there something you want to tell me?"

My brother's brows furrow, "What do you—" It hits him mid-sentence as his eyebrows relax, though his eyes grow wide for a millisecond before giving me a look. "I am not gay!"

I can't help but laugh, "Okay! I'm sorry for asking, it's just weird. I never thought you'd like—live with a bunch of guys."

"It's two guys, and they're more gay than I am."

"I am sure they are." I let my smile peek through.

"Shut up." He says as he gets out of the truck and grabs my bags from the cargo bed. I can't help but laugh now that I'm left alone, but quickly make it out before my brother snaps at me again.

I've never expected my parents' house to be turned into a bachelor pad, but I can only hope these guys have kept everything in pristine condition. I follow my brother up the steps to the front of the house and wait for him to open the door. Graves hand hesitates on the door handle, he turns to look back at me.

"Are you sure you want to do this? I feel like this is a big step you're not really thinking about."

"You're kidding, right?" I push back, "Do you know how many times I've thought about leaving Richard? Do you have any idea how long it took me to gain the strength to leave him?"

My brother sighs as he blinks twice, "Sis."

"I need this, Graves. I can't go back to that, I can't be that person again." I watch as Graves inspects my face one final time, then he turns and opens the door. When he looks back at me again, I swear I see him smile.

"I hope you find what you're looking for here, little sis." Graves grabs ahold of my hand, "This place does have the kind of magic to help you on your journey. And I mean that from personal experience."

"Yeah?"

My brother nods, "Let's go, I'll introduce you to the guys." His hand pulses around mine, we both grab one bag as we walk through the foyer and drop my bags in the front family room. I can just begin to hear the loud noises of men yelling and even the louder noise of a television, especially as my brother escorts me from one room to the next. I had expected his friends to be in the living room, which holds the largest flatscreen TV I've ever seen, but we quickly walked through the space and headed towards one of the bedrooms my parents used to have open for guests.

MIKA C.C.

Graves knocks on the door before someone yells for us to come in. I feel my heartbeat pick up, I've only ever been around Richard for a majority of my married life, meeting two new men is scary. I don't know what to expect, I don't want to be attracted to either one of them, and I also don't want them to be sleazeballs and hit on me. A small other part of me screams that this is so wrong and I should run back to Richard. I take a deep breath, or as deep as I can take, as my brother opens the door in a rush and stands in front of me like he's my bodyguard or something.

"What's up, G?" One of my new housemates asks my brother.

I only get to see the back of my brother's head, but I can imagine he's giving his friend a look, he never did well with nicknames. "Remember how we came to the agreement that we needed another roommate?"

One of them clicks their tongue, "You two agreed, if we were to get another roommate, it would be a disaster because then I'd have three of you ganging up on me when it comes to ordering fast food."

"It's not our fault you're always on some fad diet."

"Did you forget I have to watch what I eat? I'm allergic to shellfish, that's a dealbreaker, Tanner."

The other guy groans, "Whatever, I think it's just holding you back from the good stuff."

"Guys!" My brother shouts, shushing them immediately. "Can we get back to me talking?"

"Oh, I forgot, the man of the house needs to get the last word in."

Graves growls, "I'm trying to tell you assholes that the other room has been filled."

"Really?"

"Are they hot?" His two friends say simultaneously.

"I swear to god, Lucas, if you hit on her."

"A her?" Both of them speak at once.

I honestly don't know why I let them go on for so long without making my appearance, but I figured my brother had a reason for it. Now I understood, he needed to be the one to put them in their place if my living here was going to work out.

"My sister, you idiots." Graves steps aside to put me in the spotlight now. I look at both of them—the guys he called Tanner and Lucas.

Lucas is definitely the cookie-cutter California guy, I always thought they just existed in movies, but Lucas has the sunkissed skin, long, almost blonde hair, and the ever-common dark brown eyes. Tanner's skin is slightly darker, but not from the sun, his dark hair complements his skin and his eyes, they are so blue they almost compete with Richard's ocean blues. Both of them are fairly decent-looking, but once the shock wears off their faces, they both smile, and that's when I know they definitely believe they are the hottest men on the planet. They're not, though both of them have perfectly white teeth, though not all straight and some chipped. Richard still takes the number one spot as the hottest man on the planet.

After my brother quickly introduces me by name to them and does the same for Tanner and Lucas, they talk briefly about my move. My brother masterfully deviates to a different topic so I could avoid speaking of my husband. I can't seem to move from the spot I'm standing in, even though the room is huge, I feel out of place amongst the three men in one of their bedrooms. Graves doesn't seem to notice as he sits down next to Lucas and the volume of the television gets turned back up to an ungodly level of loud. Tanner invites me to sit with them on the edge of the bed, but I still don't budge. They're watching a game of hockey, which is a sport I don't fully comprehend, not when I grew up with Graves playing baseball. My brother's eyes finally glance my way, and I decide to speak, even though I hadn't in some time.

"I'm actually going to head to my room and get it set up with my things." I say, though I'm not sure I'm entirely heard over the booming of the television. So without a second for either my brother or my new housemates to speak, I leave for my room.

Chapter Three

Amelia – Present

I should've known living in a house with three men would be a bad idea. I had lived with my brother for most of my life, but the other two were a different story, and I was not prepared for them. Even as I felt at my absolute lowest, Tanner and Lucas had other plans.

The first month of living with them had been pretty easy, but only because I stuck to my room and the kitchen. The disconnect I had with the two males kept me from getting attached, but it also kept me from having real conversations. I had tried talking to my brother about my problems, but I knew he had his own problems, he didn't need to be burdened with how I felt about myself and my marriage. I buried my problem and started pretending everything was fine.

The smell of coffee every morning had wafted through my bedroom door, and every morning I'd steal a cup of the guys' coffee, usually when they were in the midst of getting ready for practice or arguing outside. They argued a lot for a group of guys that had been living together for three years.

I snuck out in my oversized sweater and cozy socks, hoping that my footsteps were hushed and my weight didn't creak on the floorboards as I made it to the kitchen to retrieve my coffee. I never had to worry about my wardrobe before, not with Richard and not with my family, so however I appeared couldn't be as bad as I thought, even with my hair tied in a high bun, half my hair falling out of the elastic. My hair had been pretty symbolic of the way my life had been going, as I let it be. I'd barely poured creamer into my coffee when a voice came from the other side of the kitchen.

"I was wondering who kept using my mug."

Lucas' voice caused my whole body to jolt as the jug of creamer slipped out of my hands and poured, not only into my mug, but all over the counter as well. I wanted to scream as my hands managed to grab the bottle now that it was half empty. The liquid left on the counter dripped off the sides nearly all over my sweater. I go to turn to grab a towel, and Lucas is next to me with two kitchen rags soaking up the creamer. He dragged the towels over to soak it up where the liquid poured from the side, just spilling more onto me. I groaned as I turned the opposite way of him and went for paper towels. I wiped the sides of the cabinet before bothering to clean up the little bit of the mess on the floor. Lucas ran to the sink to rinse the towels as I threw out the paper towels into the trash.

Both of us look up at the same time, I feel my cheeks heat as our eyes meet. Lucas smiles slightly, but I quickly look away, turning for my room before quickly remembering my coffee, I turn back to the kitchen and slip. I should've known socks on the kitchen linoleum was a bad idea. I barely have time to think about it as I feel myself fall. My body hits the ground with a large thump. Lucas quickly runs to help me up, and I feel the need to stay in this spot and think about how the world likes to make me look like a fool.

I've never been so embarrassed in my life as Lucas' hand is still waiting for me to accept his help. I let him help me up, as I only feel worse as I stand and realize how much of an idiot I must look to him, I wonder if he considers me 'Graves weird sister'. Lucas walks me over to the dining table and sits me down.

"Take those socks off before you end up with a concussion." He said quickly as he turned back to the kitchen. By the time I've slipped them off, Lucas has my coffee and walks it over to me. I didn't realize I hadn't spoken yet, until I try to say thank you, and my throat is so dry I have to clear my throat with a cough and a sip of my coffee before I'm even able to actually say the words.

"Thank you." My voice finally sounds normal as Lucas looks at me concerned.

"Are you okay?"

I chuckle to myself before I start laughing, "No." I shake my head in response before looking down at my coffee cup, "I'm not okay. I left my husband because he stopped caring. I moved back here just to live in the house I grew up in with two strangers and my brother. I have no idea what I'm supposed to do with my life, so I've been living in my depression, and to top it off, I just embarrassed the shit out of myself in front of you. My life is a complete mess, and it seems like the world is either trying to kill me or it's trying to teach me some cruel lesson."

Only when I stop speaking does Lucas sit across from me at the table. "So, that explains the wedding band."

"That's what you've taken away from everything I just said?"

15

Lucas' lips upturned, "Of course I heard everything, but I can't say we haven't been curious on why this woman with a wedding band lives in this house with us, without her husband knowing."

"Well, to start, this was my parents house first. So I should be allowed to be here without any questions from you or your friend."

"I just meant, your brother didn't tell us anything. And you've pretty much kept to yourself these last few weeks."

"What if I told you I'm more than just a mess?"

"Sounds like everyone in this house. How about this—I tell you something, you tell me something?" Lucas looks at me like he always knows what to ask.

"Do you want me to tell you why I left my husband? Is that what you want to hear?"

He shakes his head, "Whatever you want to tell me. Doesn't have to be heavy."

"You're going to start though?"

Lucas nods, "I'll make it super easy and get it out." He pauses with a deep sigh, "I'm bisexual. It's not exactly the kind of information I can let my entire team know about, but it's extremely hard to live my life the way I want when all of my teammates expect me to sleep with only women."

My view of him switches, "Wait, you're not just saying this to get me to open up to you, are you?"

"I don't even know you. I don't even care that much, but if you're going to live here, I think this would be a good place to start. And since you don't know me, you won't have to judge me or expect anything from me. Plus, the only other people that know about my sexuality are my parents and the coach."

"That's a very weird way to open yourself up to a stranger."

"I find it refreshing. Your turn." He says with a slight raise of his brow.

I take a sip of my coffee, "I left my husband. And it's not like I left in the middle of the night because he was abusive or something. He's not. Richard isn't the abusive kind. He's not even the cheating kind."

Lucas immediately looks confused, "So then, why would you leave him?"

"I got pregnant. I mean, it was over a year ago now, but it still feels fresh. I had a late miscarriage and lost the baby, it was pretty bad. I had to undergo surgery, it was—let's just say it wasn't fun." I pause to take a breath, "Everything shifted; we couldn't have sex for a while after that. I went to the doctor, who told me I had a very low chance of getting pregnant again at my age. After everything, I was where I'm at now—nearly a hundred pounds overweight, obese in under a year post surgery. Maybe I could've dealt with that on my own, but thanks to my husband being a major leaguer, paparazzi truly love to get pictures of us. Then one day I'm on a sports tabloid, being called the fattest woman to be married to one of the hottest players in the MLB."

"What?" Lucas' voice snapped.

"And it only got worse after that. I'd go to games, and I'd hear his teammates' families talk about me, behind my back but very close to my face. As much space as I take up, you'd think they'd be able to notice when I was in the same room, but I was barely visible to them. And what made me feel worse is that no one even knew why I looked the way I did. They didn't know what caused my weight gain, just that I was normal one day, disappeared for a few months, and then came back as a whole different, fatter person."

"So all of this happened—"

"In the last year, yeah. I've been dealing with bullies online, on paper, and in real life. Has my husband shut it down? Has my husband even tried to do anything about these people? Has my husband bothered to talk to me about all of it? The answer is no to each of them."

"That can't be right."

"It is. Maybe he thought I could deal with it myself, because he's so busy on the team, but he was wrong. I stopped going out, I'd decline events with him. We had an event a few months ago, and I left early because the zipper of the dress broke. I was there for maybe thirty minutes at best. And that's all it took for someone to snap a pic of me dancing with my husband, and it went viral with a caption about him dancing with a whale."

"Please tell me your husband isn't that dense? He had to have stood up for you then."

"My husband doesn't have social media. He barely goes on his phone; he barely has time for it—he barely has time for me."

"So you left because he didn't do anything."

"I left because he didn't do anything. I left because I don't even know who I am anymore. Every time I see a picture of myself, I think, that's not me. How can it be? I've never been the type of person to let one life event define me. I've never been the person who stays home because of a minor inconvenience. Ever since I've become a major leaguer's wife, I've been forced to live a public life. I thought people paid more attention to celebrities than sports players. I can't even tell you how many other pro baseball players' names I know besides you three and the Angels. Because I don't know any. Everyone knows my husband, everyone loves him. You can even look up the sexiest men alive, and he's on the list."

Lucas gasps, "I want to get on that list."

I avoid his attempt at making me smile, "On my own, no one bothers to take a picture of me. While I'm on my husband's arm? I have millions. I just couldn't. I couldn't take it anymore. I wouldn't let myself be treated like that anymore."

"That's understandable..." It's the look in Lucas' eyes that tells me how he sees me. Pitied and, worse, breakable. "Listen—"

"No. I don't need to hear a man's opinion on my body. I don't need you or anyone else pitying me. I don't want it, and I don't care for it. So whatever you're going to say, leave it elsewhere. I don't need anyone's help. I'm here because I wasn't going to let anyone else talk badly about me. I'm here because the one person I trusted more than anything, didn't have my back. I'm here because I don't know who I am anymore, who I used to be, in this house, is the me I want to get back to. I will not deal with men trying to decide what's right for me, nor will I let a man take over my life for me. So do not look at me like I'm a project, or some woman you can fix. I'm not here to fall in love with someone else. I'm here for me and me alone."

I watch Lucas' expression change before he sucks his bottom lip in between his teeth. "If you had let me talk, you would've heard me say this—I don't think I've ever met a woman who's stood up for herself. I'm a child of divorce and not even the good kind where my mom left my dad. My dad left her for another woman and demanded a divorce to marry my high school girlfriend. Yeah, you heard that right."

I don't even get the words out before he talks over me.

"I don't want to step on your toes. Hell, I'll gladly get out of your way as you take down the patriarchy. If you need help beating up your husband, I will gladly do it. I'm sure Graves would volunteer first though..."

"Graves doesn't know everything. He knows some of it, but he would kill my husband if he knew all the details."

"Graves is psychotic, so I can see that..." Lucas purses his lips together, "What about Tanner?"

"Your other roommate? What about him?"

"Can I tell him? About this stuff? I can keep a secret obviously, but I just need to know if this is like a vault of secrets to the death, or is this just a 'need to know' kind of basis?"

"Is he loyal? Trustworthy? Can Tanner keep this kind of secret?" I asked with a brow as I picked up my coffee and drink.

"Yes. One hundred percent. I'd trust Tanner with my life. Tanner is my best friend. I'd tell him my secrets in a heartbeat."

"So why haven't you?"

Lucas sucks in a breath, "I'm not sure he'd understand. On one hand, he's like a brother to me, but on the other, he'd be the first one to question my motives. How do you think you'd feel if your best girl friend was gay—the one who's seen you naked and gets drunk with you, almost weekly?"

"Are you saying that you look at Tanner's junk a lot?"

Lucas chuckles, "You are not getting me to answer that."

I smile, "I think you already did."

"Shut up!" He laughs. I can't help but giggle back at him.

"Yeah, I guess, if Tanner asks about me, you can tell him. Just make sure he doesn't tell my brother." I say with a small smile. Lucas nods as I drink my coffee.

I hear multiple knocks on my door, as I'm just waking up. After my talk with Lucas, I spent three days alone. One of my days I spent on my phone hoping to find a job, to find a therapist, and to make an appointment to a salon. I'd spent so much time not taking care of myself that it felt like the very least I could to do something just for me. I didn't care if all I did was have my eyebrows shaped up and my nails done, whatever it took to get me feeling human would be good enough for me. Though, the moment the knocks on my door turned into pounding, I felt like a machine gone mad because humans pissed me off by waking me up. If my groans weren't an answer enough to whoever was pounding on the door, my attitude was going to be. I stomped my way to the door and opened it with the force of a giant, my rage bubbling under the surface as both Lucas and Tanner stood with small smiles on their faces. One of them held a mug of coffee in one hand as the other's hands went behind their back.

"What do you want? Haven't you ever heard that women need their beauty sleep?" I asked them with a growl.

"We have, actually." Tanner answered with a small smile.

"Why are you both smiling? You realize the sun isn't even fully up yet, right?" My attitude and voice don't match up, despite me trying to sound mad at them.

"We have a proposition for you, Ames." Lucas starts.

"A good one." Tanner adds.

I roll my eyes, "Guys, it's way too early, can't you talk to me later in the day?"

"Here. Take this coffee and drink it while Tanner does the talking." Lucas takes the coffee out of Tanner's hands and gives it to me.

I take the coffee and look over at Tanner, I can tell he looks put on the spot, but he simply takes a steady breath.

"Now it might sound kind of crazy, but I have this idea. I only got the idea after Lucas told me about your problems. Really sorry about your husband being a real douche canoe. I do have a theory about that guy, but that's for another day. I want to help you. Luke does too, but only because I can't do everything myself."

"That's not true, I know some things better than you do." Lucas says to him.

"Yeah, and that's pussy. You don't know shit about the rest." Tanner says with a hand.

"Dude—"

"Bros!" I interrupt their little argument, "This isn't the time for your little pissing contest, what is this plan?"

Tanner composes himself as he looks back at me, "I actually majored in nutrition, so I am very educated in the field. I was thinking I could help you with your diet, that is if you're interested. We also have a whole gym and facility at our disposal, so Luke and I could train you. I should mention you can say no to this at any time. We just want to be on your side and help you out. If you need help with getting back out on the dating scene, we can do that too. Not us personally, but we know a lot of good-looking dudes, too. Lastly, you need friends to support you no matter what, and that's why we're standing here and not just in our beds right now."

I look over at Lucas, who seems to have agreed with everything his teammate has said. Both of them seem serious about helping me, and act like they know what they're talking about, at least Tanner does. Lucas looks like he's mainly here for moral support, but maybe I do need it. Maybe I do need more help than I let on. I sip from the mug of coffee as I look between them.

"If I say yes, does that mean I can go back to sleep?"

"Of course not!" Both of them answered.

"If you're saying yes, you need to finish that coffee, then get back in that room and change into something you can work out in. Every morning we'll be going for a run and then straight to the gym after."

I make a face of disgust as I finish my coffee, "Gross, running? In this heat?"

"You're lucky we're not having you do the workouts we've been forced to do for baseball. You do not want to lift weights the way we do." Tanner answers, shaking his head, "Cardio is just to get your heart pumping and ready for the real workout."

"I'd rather do your workout than be given some cardio and light weights."

Tanner and Lucas look at each other, an unspoken conversation sparking in their eyes before they look back at me.

"Fine." Tanner says.

MIKA C.C.

"We can teach you our workout, no problem. That just means you'll have to keep up with us." Lucas smiles.

"Then I guess you've got a deal." I say using my free hand to shake one of their hands. They both reach for my hand at once, Tanner's hand meets mine first, we shake on it, and I do the same with Lucas.

"Time for you to show us exactly who you want to be." Tanner says with a challenging glint in his eyes. I can't help but take a deep breath and smile, because I can show them and I will prove to them and myself I can get to where I want to be.

Chapter Four

Richard – Present

I'd looked at the letter way too many times. I'd never been a reader, but I used to watch Amelia read romance books like that alone was my hobby. I used to put myself in the position of the male characters she'd tell me about, never straying too far out of line for either of us, but I loved watching her blush while reading a sexy scene. I loved when Amelia would read me scenes of the man dominating the woman, I'd imagine it'd be us every time. I'd even recreate some of her favorite parts from the books. Except now that I'd read Amelia's note, I imagined it in her voice. I saw her expressions behind every word, and I imagined how I would've felt if she had said all of those things to my face. It was enough, it'd been enough to tell me to leave. I wasn't letting her go without a fight, I couldn't let the love of my life leave me like this, I couldn't let us be over. Whatever that had bothered her, everything we went through together, all of the moments that led up to this, I was there for. If she wanted to go to California, that was fine, even wanting space from me, I could understand. But, living in a completely different state, across the country from her? That I couldn't let go. That I wouldn't be able to live with.

There had been some major similarities between Florida and California weather, but the differences between the two far outweighed the similarities. After all, one state was where I met Amelia, the other state held the place with the team I planned to win the World Series with. While the humidity wasn't far off, California had one thing that Florida never truly had, and that was Amelia.

The air felt crisp the moment I stepped off the plane into the Californian sun. I had grown up in the northern parts of the state, so I felt at home. Even if my parents were living the dream of traveling the world, California still had that effect on me. Just the thought of my parents had my phone buzzing with updates from my mother herself. My phone suddenly flooded with a great big smile across my father's face in front of the Amalfi coast, along with a selfie of the two of them with my mother holding her hat down to her head, as my dad looked to be holding onto her anxiously. A chuckle escaped me for just a moment until the next text from my mom came through.

> Mom: Give Amelia our best hugs and kisses! We miss our daughter just as much as we miss our son!

I decidedly frown knowing that I can't just show the text immediately to my wife, she would know my parents still believe her to be a part of our family. The thought of my parents learning that I let Amelia run away from me, the fact that she thinks I don't care about her. My mom would kill me, and my father would disown me if they found out through anyone but me. I shake it off and text my mother back with a snarky response.

Me: I'll make sure to let Marcus and Denise know that.

Mom: Don't you dare twist my words!

Me: I would never.

Mom: If you see either of your siblings, would you tell them to pick up their phone sometime?

I hold in the smile as I realize the next part of this trip would be even harder, not only do I have to win my wife back, but I also have to beg my siblings for a place to crash. I wonder if Amelia had to do the same with her brother, Graves, but I refuse to think about it. I brush all of my recent thoughts to the side as I get in the private car I called to pick me up from the private airstrip, and immediately call my only brother, before I even think about calling my insane sister.

Amelia - Present

I pull up to my parents' little house—I say little as it's not anywhere near the style of the farmhouse I grew up in. I always knew my parents would retire and give the ranch to me or Graves, but I never pictured them leaving the house. The property they had was way larger than they knew what to do with. Besides, building a fence to reach across the nine acres to connect to the back of the house was enough for them to just let us go wild as kids. Now as I get out of my car, the house they live in is maybe twelve hundred square feet compared to the almost three thousand square foot house we grew up in.

The one thing I recognize is my dad's little pick-up truck, which both my parents have sworn has never had a bad day in the forty years he's owned it. I'm hit with a wave of nostalgia from all the times I've spent going for rides to the hardware store with my dad and Graves. It had always been the three of us working on the home projects when my mom stayed back at the ranch, cooking and taking care of the horses. I still hadn't even made it onto the ranch to see if Graves was still taking care of the same animals mom had before she retired from the "farm life".

I have to pretend this is normal. I've been so used to my life in California never changing, that coming back home like this is normal. As if coming back home as a woman separated from her husband, living with her brother and his friends in the house she grew up in, while her almost seventy-year-old parents slum it in a tiny one-story home. This is the new normal for them, but for me it's completely irrational and weird.

One minute I'm taking a deep breath, and the next I'm knocking on my parents' front door. Something I never thought I'd have to do, but the second I do, the door swings open and my mother's face goes from shocked to a soft smile. She doesn't have to do anything else as I run into her open arms. Our embrace seems to last forever, until my dad breaks the silence.

"Honey, who was—" He pauses when we both look up at him. He looks down at me with a similar smile to the one my mother initially had. "Turtle." The little term of endearment makes me smile as he wraps his arms around both me and mom.

I'm surrounded by the two people that make everything better—the two people that make these changes to my life seem insignificant. Insignificant when they don't look any older since the last time I saw them, when they smell like the same perfume and cologne for the last forty years. Nothing's changed when I'm in my parents' loving embrace.

We spent about two hours catching up in my parents' cozy living room. It has a few familiar pieces of furniture from the ranch, but it's also such a tiny space that I keep thinking that I'm bumping knees with my mom. We chuckle as my dad hands us each a cup of coffee, we'd been talking about the dog they've been fostering. They'd been happy to leave the farm animals to my brother and his friends, but they missed having a furry friend, so they'd taken up fostering dogs from the local shelter. My parents were true saints, they'd always found a way to give back to the community and always took in animals that needed rehabilitation, taking up fostering was truly no different. I should've known they weren't going to change their personalities completely just because they moved into a smaller home.

It was then that I should've noticed the quick segue brought up by my dad. Especially with the quirky little dog sleeping at the bottom of his lounge chair, a staple piece of furniture my dad would never give up. I hardly paid any attention to what my father had said when I sipped my coffee and looked at the pup's contentment next to my dad's feet. My mom's hand on my shoulder didn't even fully snap me

29

out of the zone I had on the dog, not until she tapped my shoulder twice.

"Hm? I'm sorry I missed what you said." I look at my mom quickly before focusing back on my dad.

"Things haven't gotten better with Richard?" My dad repeats, I can tell by his shoulders and the way he breathes that he's a little anxious waiting for my answer.

I shake my head, "It hasn't. That's why I'm here." I pause to look at my mom, "I'm staying in California. With Graves. Probably for a long while."

"Couples therapy didn't work?" My mom asked, she always thought it'd be helpful for us considering Richard was always on the road, and I wasn't always up for traveling with him.

"That would mean he'd have to admit we were having problems. He's always been adamant that we were fine, we just needed to communicate more."

My parents chuckle, "Therapy is a good way to communicate more." My dad says, rolling his eyes as he takes another sip of his coffee.

"So there was no trying to do anything with him. Every time I said anything, he'd dismiss me or make it seem like it was a normal part of marriage." I explained, unsure if they'd understand if I called my relationship with Richard toxic, or that he gaslighted me into staying. It never helped that he would say our life would be better once he retired from baseball. I had stopped caring and stopped asking my husband if he ever was going to put the work into our marriage.

I watch my mom rub her arm with her free hand, "That's too bad."

"Cold, honey?" My dad asks her, she's quick to shake her head, but the question is rhetorical when he gets up, setting his drink on the coffee table, to wrap her up in a blanket that was perfectly rolled in a wicker basket next to the fireplace. The second she's cocooned in the throw, she smiles, thanking him as he leans down to give her a small, soft kiss.

That was how I expected my life with Richard to be, him knowing exactly how I felt even if I tried to deny it, I shouldn't have expected him to give up baseball at thirty-nine, but we weren't getting any younger, and I hadn't exactly pictured my life as waiting for him after every practice and game at this age. I thought we'd have three kids by now, living in a house that was meant for living, not a place that reminded me of those homes from Sci-Fi movies, all white with no decor, just a bunch of computers doing the house chores for me.

"What's the plan, then?" My dad asks as he settles back into his chair with the dog's tail wagging as he jumps up on his lap. My dad lets out a chuckle as the dog licks my dad on the chin. "Oh Davey, relax, boy." He says, petting him until the dog lays perfectly still on his legs, the dog's tail wagging still but not as rapidly as before.

"Move back here." I pause, expecting a bigger reaction from my parents, but they seem to understand, "Until I'm able to afford my own place, then I'll get out of Graves way. I don't want to go back to Florida, so I'm okay with the things I left there, nothing there is important to me."

"Besides Richard." My mom says under her breath before taking a sip of her coffee. My dad and I gave her a look.

"Well, it's obvious Richard isn't giving her what she needs, hon. It's possible that her feelings for him have changed." My dad says, in a defensive tone.

"Of course." My mom says with a hand on my shoulder, "But it's not like they don't have a future together either. I mean, Ames can be here for as long as she wants, but they're always going to have this thing that connects them. We'll always be connected to his family, even if they divorce! I'm not saying this to hurt you, Turtle, but I go to yoga with his sister every Thursday. And your father is constantly running into Marcus at the hardware store."

"And the grocery store." My dad adds in. My mom points to him as if there's a point to be made.

"You'll be reminded of him even if you two don't work out, especially if you stay here."

"Mom." I start, hoping that she doesn't try and talk me out of completely walking out of my one-sided marriage.

"I'm just saying, honey. Richard is everywhere here, even when he's not here." My mom shrugged, "You've got to make peace with him before you completely give up on him."

"That doesn't make much sense to me." I say with my brows furrowed, "I'm not mad at him, I'm just done with him. Our marriage doesn't mean what it used to be to him. He doesn't—" I groan, "There are things that we don't do anymore, and I don't look the way I used to, so maybe it's me. Maybe I'm his problem the same way that he's my problem."

My parents look at each other, completely bypassing me in the middle, I turn to look at my dad and watch him look away.

"What was that?" I look between them.

"What?" My mom asks when I look straight at her.

"That look?"

"Look? There was no look, Turtle." She says, trying to gaslight me. I can see the lie written on her face.

"Mom!" She licks her lips and decides it's time for her to gather our mugs and take them to the kitchen.

"Nothing! I'll be right back!" She says in a sing-song as she's nearly running away from me.

"Dad!"

"Turtle, you know we're on your side. We believe you, we support you and love you." My dad says, with a soft smile. He sighs, "But right before you got here, we received a phone call."

"A phone call?"

"From Ramsey Senior."

"Oh. Oh god." I say as I let it sink in. My dad and Richard's dad have been friends long before we ever fell in love. I know the look on my father's face means he's regretting something.

"He said Richard was looking for you, and if we happened to see you, we'd let him know."

"I can't believe you would make a promise with another grown man. Hello? We're adults, we don't have to act like teenagers and keep promises to our best friends. You keep it to yourself, dad."

"I want to, I really do, Turtle. Ramsey and I just have this—"

"Dad! Daughter trumps best friend! Do you get that? My privacy comes first." I can't believe I have to explain this to my seventy-something-year-old dad.

"You're right, I know..." He trails off, distracting himself with the dog on his lap. I roll my eyes and feel my teeth grit together as I remember my dad sucks at keeping secrets. I groan as I come up with a plan in my head.

"Fine. You can tell Ramsey Senior, but you have to wait a week or so. I just got here, I need to find my bearings first. I need to figure out what the heck I'm going to say to Richard if he shows up here." I run through the rest in my head. I can already picture Richard making his surprise appearance, and expecting me to drop everything to go back to Florida with him. I can't let it happen. One week should work for me to find a job and maybe enough time for me to coerce my brother to get rid of the two guys living in our old guest rooms, so we can just take over the farm the way my parents expected us to.

"Okay. I think I can do that." My dad gives me a tight smile.

"Not think, dad. You're going to. Remember, daughter comes first."

Goodbyes in my family always take three hours. By the time I'm leaving my parents house, it's almost midnight. I finally walk out my parents front door, breathing a breath of fresh air. They are one part of this I don't have to worry about. My parents have always been on my side, but it's nice to have had time to explain everything to them in person. After everything, it's refreshing to get it all off my chest.

Between the time it takes for me to walk from their front door to my car, I watch as a sleek black car pulls up on the curb next to my parent's mailbox. I'm fairly certain their visitor is not welcome at nearly midnight, so I start walking towards the car when the rear driver's side door opens. I take a couple steps back as I register the legs that get out of the car, and then the man that stands there with an almost scowl on his face.

"Richard." I breathe out, all the fresh air seems to have evaporated when my husband's scent is the only thing that fills my nostrils. The car door slams, and I nearly jolt at the sound. As he takes a step forward, I take one back. Despite his permanent frown, Richard seems just as shocked to see me.

There's nothing I have to say to him, not now anyway. I told my dad that I had needed time to think, and I still do. I try to busy myself by looking away, but only at the driver who's now pulled out Ramsey's luggage and set it next to him. Three suitcases sit by his feet. Three. How long does he think he's going to be here? I've never seen my husband pack for longer than a three-day trip, and even then his things are usually packed in a small, hard-covered suitcase.

"You don't have to say anything now. But I just wanted to say I'm not leaving."

Those are the only words I hear from my husband's mouth, I'm sure he said more before, but between the distraction of his luggage and the sounds of the crickets singing in the distance, I'm left rather speechless. I guess it hadn't mattered what I told my dad not to say to Ramsey Sr., not when Richard's standing in front of me, less than five feet away.

"Um." I stammer out, "At my parents house?"

Richard sighs, "I didn't give anyone a heads up, and your parents were the only ones to answer my texts."

My eyebrows raise in question, "You texted them? When?"

"About an hour ago." He answers with his brows furrowed as he takes a step closer to me. I take a step back, right into the back of my car. I'd assumed he would retreat from me trying to create space between us, instead, Richard runs a finger across my twisted brows.

"Richard, what are you—?" I whisper as he repeats the motion before stepping away.

"I'll be seeing you around, my love." The words he says tumble around in my brain as I watch him find a way to grab all three suitcases and walk with them up to my parents door. The black sleek car drives away, as I look back at my husband with the door slightly opened and my parents just on the other side as he waves lightly at me.

My forehead hurts just from me frowning so much, and I'm left to get back in my car and drive back to the ranch and pretend like my husband isn't temporarily living with my parents. Now he gets to tell them his side of the story, a side I have yet to hear myself...

Chapter Five

Amelia – Past

AMELIA (12), RICHARD (14)

I have to speed walk to reach my mom at the stables. After my dad had told me that she needed my help with the horses, I expected a lot more than seeing my mom setting up the saddle on Calliope. I groan as I finally make it to her, I should've known my dad was trying to put me to work.

"Hey Turtle, what are you doing out here?"

I feel my cheeks heat, more than they already feel from the trek out. "Dad told me you needed me."

"Oh." My mom says going back to fitting the bridle to the horse. "Oh, I see... Well, follow me then." She winks at me as the little smile on her face tells me she's up to no good. I follow her, occasionally looking at her like she's a goddess. It doesn't help that the sun just makes her look more radiant, she was constantly told she was Cameron Diaz's doppelganger, which was incredibly believable despite my mom always being very humble about the resemblance.

I look back at Calliope as my mom and I get closer to the gate. This horse has always had a problem with riders, but my mom is stubborn enough to get the mare to follow her direction.

"Don't you think it's a bad idea to put her with strangers?" I ask as I feel Calliope stare back at me. I swear the mare is telling me to save her from hurting someone.

"She has to get over this. She knows every Tuesday is horse camp."

"Mom, she's a horse!"

"Turtle, Callie is the only horse that has been through this trauma, the only way for her to get through it, is to keep trying. You'll learn all about this when you get older, I'm sure. But this is what's best for her."

I click my tongue together as my mom opens the gate and ushers in the families. My mom immediately goes into tour guide mode. She tells them what ranch life is like, what it's like to own farm animals, and that everywhere their eyes can see is a place for the animals to free roam. We've tried to be very inclusive and helpful to any and all farm animals. She even goes into detail about the few animals we've rehabbed and are currently rehabbing. Calliope being one of them.

The families ooh and ahh like they've never learned the culture before, despite growing up in a very farm-rich town. My parents ranch has always been one of the four main farms for just about everything. While we've tried to expand it to just about anything and everything, they made a deal with the neighboring farms that they'd offer the horse-riding lessons and horse camp. Most of the farms had the cattle and chickens to sell products, and two of them offered handling and care classes for the farm animals, but that was the extent of their education. My mom decided the horses were what would separate their farm from the rest. They were right and my mom made a killing at it when my dad was constantly working at the auto shop.

My mom pulled me into her side and chuckled, "And this is Amelia. We call her Turtle around here because she and her brother used to race. And if you ever heard of the story of the turtle and the hare, that was them. Can you guess which animal she was?" My mom asks, still giggling while most of the kids my age don't seem amused.

One kid raises his hand as my mom picks on him, "Isn't it the tortoise and the hare? Shouldn't her nickname be tortoise then?"

My mom's jaw drops, and then she closes it, "Oh, I suppose you're right. We always told it as the turtle because Amelia's brother never could pronounce tortoise with that hard r sound."

This time I chuckle as I reminisce on my big brother having to go to speech therapy because of his trouble pronouncing words with hard R's. My mom overhears my laugh and smacks my butt. I stiffen and feel my cheeks heat around the other kids.

"Today, Amelia and I are going to introduce you to our mare, Calliope. She's a great girl, she just needs to be around some people today." I give my mom a look as she loud-whispers her last sentence to the group. I let her walk ahead of me as I try to imagine why she's singling Callie out, and why on earth she needs to be around people. Meanwhile, I overheard the conversation between the boy who called the turtle the tortoise and his mom.

"I can't believe you just called out that woman like that, Richie. Goodness, I thought I taught you better manners." The mom's chuckle is hidden by the scoff in her voice.

"Maybe if you took me to baseball camp instead of this crap, I'd have better manners."

"Richard!" His mom scolds, "You will not talk like that here. You need a break from that nonsense. You know baseball isn't life, right? You need to have other hobbies than just a ball and a bat."

"It's not just a ball and a bat, mom!" I hear the kid get angry and notice that the closer we get to Callie, the more she'll be able to read the emotions of these two and will copy what they're feeling, and it will end badly.

"Hey!" I say turning around and running closer to the kid. He's definitely my age, maybe slightly older by his height, but his eyes are such a light blue that I almost fall as I get closer to him.

He must see me trip on my own two feet because his arms are right there to catch me, "You good?"

"Yeah." I say with a little grin, "You like apples?"

"What?" He looks taken off guard by my question. Maybe he thinks I'm about to land a horrible joke because the look on his face screams confused.

"The horses, they love apples. There's one horse that even does tricks with them. Want to see?"

"What kind of tricks?"

"Are you good at throwing a ball?"

He chuckles, "You could say that."

"Follow me, I won't lead you astray." I smile, outstretching my hand to him.

"Do I have to hold your hand?"

"I guess not, but we'd get there faster that way." I try to hide my already large smile, he takes my hand anyway, and we run for the stables.

"Turtle!" I hear my mom yell as I run past her with the kid, Richard, in tow.

We're catching our breaths once we make it into the stables. The sun peeks through the wooden boards, and even though it's pretty dark in the stables, there's still streaks of light that the horses gravitate towards. I show Richard where we keep the horses snacks, in a cupboard they can't get to. Technically, the cupboard is supposed to be for cleaning supplies for their manes, but me and my brother were always on horse duty, so instead, we ended up stocking and replenishing the snacks in the cupboard.

Diamond turns when I call her, and Richard looks completely scared of her, almost like he's out of his depth being alone with me and a horse.

"I promise she won't hurt you." I say with a cheesy smile.

"Yeah, right. She's staring daggers at me right now."

I burst out laughing, "Diamond? She's everyone's favorite horse. She's the one that should be out there with the group, not Calliope."

"Why not Calliope?" He asks with furrowed brows.

"Well—" I shrug, "Long story short, she had a bad human. He didn't know how to take care of her, and she just got weary of humans. We were lucky that she took to us the way we found her."

"What's the long version?"

I pressed my lips together, "Callie is just very skittish, her owner just didn't give her enough attention, and when he rode her, he used a whip instead of reins. He was a jerk. We literally found her on the side of the road with her bridle still on her and the saddle hanging off her side. It took us six months for her to even warm up to the saddle."

"Shit."

MIKA C.C.

My eyes grow wide at Richard's choice of words.

"What? My bad word?" He rolls his eyes at me as I nod, "Don't horses parrot behavior or something?"

"Uh yeah. What does that have to do with your curse word?"

Richard clears his throat, "I parrot my dad. He curses a lot. So when mom's not around, I say bad words. Though, I wish they'd let me curse already."

"How old are you?"

"Fourteen. You?"

"You're my brother's age. I'm twelve."

"Who's your brother?"

"Graves. You probably don't know him."

He nods his head, "Everyone knows who Graves is. He's the only kid at school with that name."

I chuckle, "Fair point."

Chapter Six

Amelia – Present

"What do you think you're doing?" I hear my husband's voice before I can even stand up from my seat on the front porch.

"Ramsey..." I say with a straight face, hoping he leaves as quickly as he appeared.

"Amelia!" His deep crackle of a yell caused me to straighten and look up at him. "Why the hell are you wearing that jersey?"

I glare at him, harder than I ever have before. He seems to do the same, causing me to keep up my guard. I've never been more mad at him, I've never felt such anger toward my own husband before.

My brother seems to cut the tension with his entrance, "So I found the—" he stops when his eyes meet with Ramsey's. Both of them are so broody and naturally grumpy you'd think they'd be the ones related.

"Graves."

"Richard." Ramsey gives my brother a hardened look, "Ramsey." Not even Graves can hold out from the intimidation my husband gives off.

Ramsey looks back at me, "The jersey needs to come off."

"That's my jersey." Graves points to himself, "I gave it to her."

Ramsey growls in response.

"She can wear my jersey when she's visiting me, especially when she's here to get away from *you*."

"Amelia wouldn't do that."

"She's fine wearing my number."

Ramsey growls again.

"Doesn't *she* get a choice or a say?" I ask, since they're speaking of me like I'm not in between them.

"No." Both of them speak simultaneously.

"Fuck both of you." I say under my breath, both of them give me dirty looks. I stand and hope to god one of them will get why I'm putting space between them.

"Make a move toward my sister, Dick."

"I'm her husband."

"That's not what I heard."

Richard's eyebrows raised at my brother's words, but his eyes searched for me, "What did you hear?"

"That you learned to fuck off a long time ago."

"That is not what I said." I give Graves a look of dissatisfaction. My brother rolls his eyes and shrugs.

"Close enough to me." My brother says with a smirk.

"Amelia, what the fuck is this clown talking about? Does he know that *you* left me?"

Graves can't help but laugh, "You've got to be kidding me." Ramsey's eyes darken every time they flit to my brother, but the second they come back to me, I swear they glisten.

"Richard, you left me long before I left you."

"I never left you, Amelia."

My brother's laughter is fake, and the sound reminds me of every time he used to beat anyone that tried to gaslight him to believe they didn't bully me.

"That's rich coming from you." My brother's voice gets deeper, I can feel him holding back from punching Richard's lights out.

"Amelia, please."

With a quick look at my brother, he takes a hesitant step back, "Let me handle this, please."

"I can take him for you," Graves says, but with another look he understands, then looks at my husband, "I'll be right inside, able to hear everything, so if I need to, I'll have your ass on the grass before I even make it onto the porch."

"You can't even make a homerun, you expect me to believe you can have me on my ass when you can't even reach the second plate?"

Now my brother chooses his moment to growl at Richard, "Graves, he's doing it on purpose. Please, go inside." The look between the two of them is a road of fury I can only imagine they'd take if a single tear sprang loose from my eyes. With that, my brother finally secedes and takes silent, shallow steps until he's inside. I have no idea where he planted himself, but I can only imagine he's not far from the door, so he can easily come if I were to yell. Protective brothers are the best.

"Can we talk about what happened?" Ramsey asks with a look on his face, it's one I haven't seen in so long, it's almost unbelievable that it took me flying to California for him to look at me the way he is.

"Sure." I gesture towards the porch swing for him to sit down. When he takes his seat in the middle of the swing, I realize I'm forced to sit on either side of him, having no space to keep us apart. Ramsey did it on purpose, to feel close to me, even if we're separated on every other level.

"I want to understand why you left me. Again." He says as I finally take my seat next to him, I feel my chest tighten when his hand falls and rests on my knee. Our skin touching shouldn't have any effect on me anymore, but it still does, especially after spending weeks away from him.

"Nothing changed, again, Richard."

"I'm trying, Ames. I was trying," He turns his head to face me, but even I can't look him in the eye anymore than I already have. If I do, I'll break.

"In all the wrong ways." A warm breeze flows through the porch and my hair, my skin reacts with goosebumps, nothing about it is right, and it just reminds me of him, of us. "We don't fit like we used to, you don't make me feel like I used to."

"Oh." I can only see Ramsey through my periphery, but I watch as he turns away and hangs his head. "So you don't... You don't love me anymore?"

"It's complicated, Richard."

"Is it? You just made it sound pretty clear that you don't."

I finally look at him as he looks down at his hands, I feel my eyes water, "I'll always have love for you. You were my first love, you were my first everything. I'm not going to forget that. We just grew apart. You grew with your team rather than with me. You chose baseball over saving our marriage."

Ramsey pulls his head up to look back at me, "I never would've. If I could, I'd go back and choose you. I've always chosen you before."

"You know that's not true."

"When have I not chosen you, Amelia? You're my world."

"Baseball is your world, I've always come second. Getting to the World Series has always been your number one. I traveled with you to Florida, away from my family, so you could get there. And you did, and at what cost?"

"So I could retire and be with you."

"Look at how well that worked out." I chuckled, with less than a smile.

"You left before I had a chance to—"

"I gave you time, I gave you plenty of it. I saw you on that field, I watched the whole game, you're not ready to give it up."

"That doesn't matter, Amelia. I made you a promise. The glove has been hung up."

"Has it? How sure are you?" I ask, searching his face for value, for truth, and for so much more.

"What do I need to do to prove to you that you're what's most important to me?"

"Richard," I pause, still searching his expression, and finding that he still doesn't understand. "I need you to go home, back to Florida."

"My home isn't in Florida." Richard chokes out.

"I need time, and that time needs to be spent away. Away from you."

"You really don't want to be with me, do you?"

I look away and rub the tears that stain my cheeks. I take a deep breath; if he only knew, "I need to figure out who I am without you, Richard. You need to figure out what you want outside of baseball. If I'm still what you want in a year, then we can revisit this. Us."

"A *year*? You're putting a year's worth of space between us? We're still married, Amelia."

I give him a sharp look, "For now. A lot can change in a year, not enough can in six months. I'm not being unreasonable, I don't think."

Ramsey takes a deep breath, daring to look angry at me, "Fuck. I can't believe I'm agreeing to this." His pause is confusing before he continues, "But if it helps us getting back to us, I'll do it."

My brows raise, "Really?"

"I said I'd do anything for you."

I take a moment before I decide how to react, settling on a quick hug, but the second I wrap my arms around him, our mouths are crashing together. Ramsey's mouth tastes of spearmint and coffee. Our tongues and lips stay together until I finally pull away, just reliving the memory of our first kiss on this swing makes me want to stay where we are, though I know if we do, we'll stay the same people getting lost in our marriage.

Our lips separate in time for me to see tears swell in my husband's eyes, but they disappear the moment he blinks.

"I guess this is goodbye." The moment the words leave my mouth, I feel the emotion in my chest, my voice, and my eyes. Whether he gets it or not, the truth is that we're separating, and I have no doubts that this separation will be the end of our marriage. Richard shakes his head, "Not really. I mean, it is a goodbye, but it's not *our* goodbye. This is just—well, I don't know what it is, but this is not our ending."

I feel my eyes well with tears again, but the more I look at him, the more I know he's remaining positive and hopeful for the both of us.

"This is not how our story ends." He says with finality as he looks at me. I watch as Ramsey plasters on a fake smile as he stands, "I'll see you soon, my love."

Chapter Seven

Richard – Past

AMELIA (14), RICHARD (16)

After two summers spent at Graves and Amelia's family ranch, I had finally reached the age where I was thinking of girls as more than just friends. Graves had been the first of the guys on our school baseball team, to have a girlfriend. And maybe it was seeing him walk around school with a girl's hand in his, that made me think it was time to find a girl to be interested in. Throughout the school year I had thought I'd be into one of the girls I went to school with, but no matter the class or being paired up with a female counterpart, I felt no attraction.

It was a walk in the park for me to talk to just about anyone, but I didn't feel comfortable talking about everything, not when my classmates would talk about going on winter vacation to different countries, especially when they talked about visiting family out of state. Which was a sensitive topic for me as a young teenager.

My parents were the last living relatives of everyone in their respective families. They'd found each other in the throes of their own depression; my dad's brother had passed a week before and my mother's dad passed the day before. Despite it all, they stayed in contact, and they'd have multiple random meets before they decided to try dating. My mom called it 'unfortunate lucky encounters', because more than half of the times they'd seen each other, they were at a family member's funeral. Once the two of them started dating, they made it their plan to stick together and have a big family. Three siblings wasn't too big in my opinion, but my parents suggested otherwise, and there were enough of us to bother each other, so we stopped asking for another sibling.

By my third summer, I felt like I'd known the ranch well enough to be calling out the names of all of the farm animals. I had walked out to the wooden fence and waved a quick bye to my mom, while she drove off with my youngest siblings to another summer camp for their age group. The moment I made it over to the barn where all the kids had gathered, the second Mrs. Evans sees me and I watch a large smile take over her face. It reminded me of an actress' smile, but I didn't pay much attention to TV to remember names.

"Hi, Richard. Nice to see you again." Mrs. Evans says as she looks like she's trying not to smile too much at me. I want to cringe at her calling me by my first name, but I have to remember she's not a regular figure in my life for her to know that I go by Ramsey everywhere else.

"You can call me Ramsey, if you want, Mrs. Evans." I say with a small smile. My voice causes long brunette hair to whip from in front of me, the girl in front of me turns. I knew her from school, but her name escaped my mind.

"Ramsey Greene?" The girl interrupts Mrs. Evans before she's even able to get a word out.

"Yeah?" Confusion laces my voice, but I don't know what else to say.

"Sienna. Jones. We've had classes together since, like, first grade." The girl's brown eyes look familiar, and I'm sure she's right, but as forgettable as she is, I'm caught up by the girl that trots by on my favorite horse. Callie neighs as both her and Amelia's hair flies in the wind until she stops her. A quick trollop and stop, Amelia hops down, and I swear she looks like a completely different girl. I gulp, trying not to stare as she dismounts the horse and heads to her mother. I've hardly paid attention to the girl speaking to me, but I can still hear her high-pitched voice droning on about how I should know her. It doesn't even matter, not when Amelia puts her long hair up in a quick ponytail, busy talking to her mom, not even realizing I'm staring at her. I'm staring at her body, her newly sprouted body parts that she didn't have last year.

"That's my sister, perv." I feel a shove as I look at my side to see Graves glaring at me.

"Oh hey, Graves! Ha. It's like a reunion." Sienna chuckles. I finally look at her and realize she's always been the girl who followed Graves around like a lost puppy in grade school.

"Sienna, right. Now I remember." I say stupidly. She rolls her eyes at me and chuckles,

"It's about time." I focus solely on Graves now, surely he gets why I looked at his sister when Sienna hasn't stopped talking since either of us said a word to each other. It only takes another few minutes of Sienna's incessant voice for Amelia to turn around to see who's talking. Amelia's hazel eyes meet mine for a mere second before she looks towards her brother, it only takes her a few steps and she's at Graves side.

I wish I could look straight at Amelia, but more people start crowding around her and her brother. I've already lost the nerve to say a simple hello, not that it would come out any different in front of her brother, but because I want one-on-one time with her. I let the other kids our age talk to Amelia and Graves, and I swear I can't see a lick of resemblance in the two of them, despite them having the same parents. I always wondered if the Evans family had a secret they didn't want shared with the rest of the world, especially since Amelia and Graves didn't even attend the same school. As soon as the thought crosses my mind, Amelia's eyes find mine, she looks bored the second I scan her face. Maybe she's not a people person like me, but the second another person starts talking to her, she warps her face into a grin. One I can only hope is fake, when I realize it's my next-door neighbor, Kyle.

"How's the summer treating you?" I hear him say, and that's all I need to bustle in between the small crowd of teens, to her side.

"It's been good, thanks for asking." I answer Kyle, almost out of breath.

"Rams. Where did you come from?" He chuckles nervously. Kyle has always been the one to chase after what I want, between baseball and friendships, he's been trying to one-up me in every way. Amelia is no different, I can see it in his eyes. Even though I know he loves to challenge me, I can tell that he's also intimidated by me, with the way he shrinks into Amelia.

Amelia looks between us and chuckles, "My summer has been just fine. You know how it is living on a farm, don't you?" She asks both of us. Neither of us live on a farm, but we smile and nod like we know all about it. This might be Kyle's first summer on the ranch, but it's not mine, so at least I can ask more in-depth questions.

"How's Callie?" I quickly ask before Kyle can get a word out.

Amelia's smile shines, "She's doing great. Are you planning on kidnapping her this year?"

"It's not my fault she loves me more than you."

"Oh? We'll see about that. I've been giving her a lot more attention this year."

"I'm sure you have, but you know what they say."

"What do they say?" Amelia asks with furrowed brows, as eager as she is, I can tell she's curious too.

"Horses love an alpha." I smirk at her. Amelia chokes out a laugh.

"You're kidding, right?"

"You don't think I'm an alpha?"

"An alpha asshole maybe." She teases.

I hear a laugh come from my side, and I look over briefly, to see that Kyle is still standing next to us, as if he's a part of our conversation. When I look back at Amelia, she seems to have a new expression while looking at Kyle, her head turns back to me, and she hums. That hum, that noise, I swear it was just for me.

"You wanna take a walk with me to see Callie?" Amelia asks, and it's the only thing I need for me to follow her and leave Kyle in the dust behind us.

Part of me had wished I didn't follow Amelia and just stuck with the group this time around, but I swore I learned more from her than what Mrs. Evans taught all fifteen of us. I had every intention of following the rules, but once I was on the field, grass or dirt, I felt free and like I knew exactly where to go. On this field, I knew to follow Amelia's footsteps.

"What?" Amelia asked me with a small smile gracing her face.

"What?"

She chuckled, "You were staring at me."

I shook my head, "Sorry. It's just... It's been a year since I saw you last."

"Yeah, and?"

"You look... You look different."

Her brows furrowed, "Different good or different, bad?"

"Good! Definitely good!" My heart thumped loud enough to tell me I didn't have to get so loud with my answer, but even I knew that was impossible. I felt my cheeks heat, embarrassment was not my best look, but Amelia seemed to laugh at me. With us under the shade of the barn, I hoped the pink of my cheeks didn't show. It wasn't until we met in the middle of the horses stables, that I noticed her red cheeks.

"You look different, too, you know."

"I do?" I ask, feeling my heart beat even faster.

Amelia hums in response, "I never would expect you to have a five-o'clock shadow at sixteen."

I chuckled, "It only just started happening." With my eyes still on her, I watch reluctance in her stance, like she's afraid of getting closer. I'm afraid of getting closer, too, but it's not because of her, it's because of what I'd do if I had the chance to touch her. To feel her soft skin beneath the pads of my fingers, to be close enough to smell her aroma and figure out exactly what her natural scent is. I just know if I touch her, I might never want to let go.

"You're staring again."

"Why do you look scared? Do I scare you?"

"Wh-what? No. You don't scare me." She says with a slight chuckle in her voice. "Okay, now you really expect me to believe that?"

Amelia lets out a smile I've never seen before, taking a few steps closer to me, "I promise, I'm not scared of you."

"Then what are you scared of, little Turtle?" I watch her eyes flick down to my lips before they look back up at me.

"Um. I don't know. Maybe foxes?"

"Foxes?"

"Because they kill the chicken and steal the eggs."

"So you wouldn't consider me your fox, would you?"

A breath of a chuckle escapes her mouth, "No. You're just a rooster."

"I feel like I should ask why you think I'm a rooster." I say with a laugh.

"You should!" Amelia laughs back.

"But I really want to kiss you first."

Amelia's eyes grow wide, "You want to kiss me?"

"I do. I mean, I won't if you don't want me to..."

"No. I do. I want you to kiss me. Like, ever since I met you, it's what I've wanted."

I can only assume I look shocked, but her words hit me twice before they hit me again, and the third wave brings my body closer to hers. Under the barn, we're secluded from everyone, minus Callie and the two foals that were born a few weeks ago. The shade keeps us from being seen, the air around us is thick, with need, with want to kiss each other. We're both young and inexperienced.

Part of me hoped that I'd have my first kiss with someone other than Graves' sister, especially since we've been in competition for the spot of center fielder on our school's baseball team. Though the thought escapes me the second my lips touch Amelia's, I've never thought I'd have something to look forward to every summer, but Amelia has become just that. Kissing her is like passing second and third base, like the ball is out of the park, and the home run is as easy as it is natural. Amelia's lips feel like they were meant for mine, her body wrapped around mine is like the adhesive side of a sticker sticking to where it belongs. I never thought my first kiss would feel so addictive, but I should've known better, everything about Amelia makes me want her. Someone in DARE should've taught me how addictive Amelia's kisses are.

When our lips part, I'm the first to open my eyes and watch her lips contort back to normal. I don't think I've ever been this close to her before, but now that we're this close, I'm inspecting every pore, every breath, and every noise that comes from Amelia. Her eyes open, and she blinks those pretty hazel eyes, and the only thought to pass is how she is the definition of perfection.

Chapter Eight

Ramsey – Present

"Hello? Did you hear me at all?" I pop the gum in my mouth and pull myself together, looking at the horses' barn reminds me of my start with Amelia.

I can hear Christian's breath over the phone, "I'm fine." I answer quickly before he can yell at me.

"That was not the question. Guntz has been asking for you. Cap and I can only cover you for so long."

"Yeah, well, I might not be coming back."

"Wait, don't hang up yet." I actually find myself shocked that Christian knows me that well, but maybe it's the combination of him and Lane calling me for the past four days that has them knowing my next move.

"What?" I ask with my gum grinding in between my teeth. I haven't even begun to get fed up with their calls, but I do lose my patience talking with any of my teammates.

"Can you at least tell me why you're not in Florida?"

"It's personal, Hayes."

"So wait, you can give me advice on my relationship with Madison. You and Cap can hug about Nova's pregnancy, but you can't give us anything about you running away to California?"

"Well, Cap and I did not hug."

"That's what you're focusing on?"

"Why would I hug that maniac?"

"Dude. Please, give us something we can tell Guntz."

I let a long silence pass between us before I finally answered, "I'm fixing my mistakes."

Another long silence passes in our phone call, "I get it." Christian's voice sounds almost shaken, "Trust me, out of everyone on the team, I get it. Guntz won't, and I'm sure Cap won't either, but I do."

I sigh, "Hayes." Ready to explain my situation to someone who might actually relate despite the difference in our age. Christian would be the one guy to understand, he's been one of a few guys to keep a girlfriend throughout his time in the league. I've thought about who I would tell all of my secrets to, and it's always been Amelia, but having to rely on someone else, if it were anyone, maybe Christian Hayes would be the friend I'd need... Though as soon as I see Amelia exit the barn, all of my thoughts disappear.

"Yeah?"

"I gotta go." I hang up the phone before he has a chance to say anything else. Maybe another day I'll explain it to him. Amelia still looks as perfect as the first day I met her, the first time I kissed her, and all of our other firsts.

I watch Amelia roll her eyes the second she sees me. Her hair blows in the wind as she storms past me, shaking her head. I grab her arm and watch as she turns to look at my hand placement on her.

"What do you think you're doing?" She asks with a bite behind her words.

"Me?" I ask with raised brows, "What are you doing, getting angry at me for?"

"I have every right to get angry at you."

"No, you don't, Amelia. You left me."

"This, again?" She scoffs, folding her arms over her chest.

"Do you really want to yell about this out here?"

"Yes! I do! I don't understand why you followed me out here. I don't understand why you're here, you have games, don't you?"

"You think I can play knowing you're out here, doing god knows what, while living in a house with your brother who hates me and two other guys?"

Amelia laughs, "That's fucking rich coming from you." She tries to run, but I catch her other arm as she pulls herself out of my grasp.

"Me? What did I do?"

"What didn't you do, Richard? I'm so tired of having to spell it out for you." Amelia turns as if ready to walk away from me.

"Dammit, Amelia. I'm here." She turns at my words, her worry lines above her brows showing, though I can tell she's equally as confused. "I'm not on the other side of the country anymore. I'm right here, I'm fighting. Fighting for you. Can't you even tell?"

Amelia looks away from me for multiple seconds before she turns to face me, tears streaking down her face, "You shouldn't be fighting for me. You shouldn't even be here." I swear I hear her hum with the way she looks at me, "Go home, Richard. Please."

It's as if the sky agrees with her, as a light drizzle of rain begins, it's not nearly enough to soak her hair or my clothes, but it's enough for me to let my disappointment show on my face without her noticing the expression. The rain is enough to let tears escape from my own eyes, because I have no home. Without Amelia, I have no home.

Chapter Nine

Amelia – Present

I've cried too long and too often over Richard, for him now to be in my space and working on the ranch with me, is honestly too much. The last time I saw him, I almost dropped my guard, but the moment he opens his mouth is when I know he's here for the wrong reasons. I'm glad I haven't given him any part of me, it's only been a few months since the last time I slept with him and only a few months of being away from him, but I can tell Richard won't relent. He's not the kind of person to stay away, perhaps that's why we were together for so long in the first place. Neither of us had time to explore other relationships, neither of us dared to even break up when we were younger. There was something about Richard that even from a young age, I was attracted to, maybe not physically, but we clicked together and not like the stereotypical peas in a pod, but the way magnets pull toward one another, but when faced the other way, pull apart. The only difference between Richard and me is that I'm the only one facing the other way, he's still looking at me, hoping our magnetism will be enough to keep us together.

It's been a week and I've seen Richard come and go from the fields all day, I've watched him gather up hay and bring it out to the stables, and feed the chickens with no problem. Well, maybe there is one tiny problem, and that problem is, he's been doing all of it shirtless. I knew pretty early on that he was doing it to get my attention, so I let him. Richard does all the dirty work, and I mean literally—cleaning up the horse poop and getting attacked by the hangry chickens, among other various ranch hand duties. While I've decided to sit on the porch and enjoy the view. Most of the time I've been distracted by housework to really even have time to sit and enjoy, but on a day where it looks like rain, I've decided to enjoy my tea and a good book on the porch swing.

It's when I hear a phone ring, that I look up from my book. When I brought it out, I was just at the beginning, but now having a moment to put a bookmark in between the pages, I realized I'm almost finished. I quickly get up and search for the phone, the phone that might be mine, since I never brought it out with me. Since I've been here, I've needed my phone less and less, and now that Richard's here, it's even better to avoid my phone altogether. When I finally found the phone, the ringer started and stopped three times. When I pick up the phone, I'm forced to look at the shirt that was underneath it. It takes no time for me to realize whose phone it is, but I still stare at the screen when it rings again. I still look at the background with our wedding picture, it feels like a lifetime ago and like it was yesterday all at the same time. The number calling pops up for a fifth time, and this time I finally answer it.

"Hello?" I say carefully.

"Amelia?" A familiar voice calls on the other line. I've realized I've made a huge mistake picking up Richard's phone, but it's too late now.

"Roman. Hey."

"Well, this is a happy surprise. Things must be going—"

"Roman, this is not a happy surprise. As much as you may hope this is the type of call that someone may answer from a night together, it is not. Richard is out mowing the lawn."

"He's mowing the—you're letting Ramsey mow the lawn? Why is he mowing a lawn at all? He's supposed to be winning you back." I can't help but let a smirk cross my face, as I walk with the phone back to my seat.

"Maybe he thinks he can win me back by mowing the lawn."

"Woman, you know damn well that is not the way a man wins back his wife's heart." Roman says with a snap to his words, "Plus, in what universe have you or I ever expected Ramsey to ever mow a lawn?"

"What if I told you he's also picking up horse shit?"

"Amelia Shae Greene, he better not be." I chuckle despite Roman's tone. It feels like old times talking to Richard's agent. We used to get together with Roman and his wife every few weeks, most of it was for the guys to talk baseball and deals, but I had somewhat of a friendship with Claire. I had to put the thought of Claire to the back of my thoughts, knowing she had been part of the reason for most of my problems. I never took out my anger on Roman since he didn't know any better, but he was the first one I told once the media started doing what they do best.

"You still there?" Roman's voice trills through the phone.

"Yeah," I answer with a nod, "I'm just..."

"It's going to get better. I mean, I know you don't want him there, but he's not leaving without you. I only called to see how things were going for him."

"Yeah. I get that."

"How are you, though? Are you getting... Help? I'm sure Ramsey's told you, but Claire and I. Well, we're taking a break."

My eyes grow wide despite having seen it coming, "What did Ramsey say about that?" The silence on Roman's end of the phone, along with his sigh, was enough to tell me, but I waited to hear from him.

"He said he was sorry, but didn't pry for information. You know how he is with people. He doesn't get involved—"

"That's part of the problem, Roman. He never gets involved. He never asks what's the problem, he never thinks to consider that he might have something to do with the issues. Does he even talk about the paparazzi? Did he even tell you about—" I start to lose my nerve with the onslaught of tears that fall from my eyes, a sob escapes me. I can't even get the words out, no matter how hard I try.

"I'm sorry, Ames. Truly, I wish I had more to tell you. I only know because of you. And well, I just wish things had gone a different way."

I wipe away my tears with my free hand, "Yeah, me too." I switch hands with the phone and clean up the rest of my wet face. "He deserves to be shoveling shit and throwing around hay."

"Yeah, but I bet it's only making him look sexier without the shirt on, doesn't it?" Roman's voice sounds playful in his question. I'm unsure if he wants to hear the truth, but I let it slip anyway.

"He really does. It's not fair... I mean, it's really not fair, Roman."

"I know, hon. I'd give you a hug if I could."

"And you'd get a smack on the head if you dared to try to hug me." I chuckle with a grin spread across my lips.

MIKA C.C.

Roman laughs on the other line, I haven't been paying attention to the field or my book in so long that I don't realize the shade that has covered me isn't from the house.

"Is that my phone?" I was startled by the sound of Richard's voice and almost dropped his phone in the process. One hand grabbed the phone while the other clutched my chest.

"Jesus, Richard. A little warning next time?" I say as I look up and see his sweaty bare chest on display for me. I have to take a gulp of dry air to pretend like I'm not checking my husband out.

"Have you been sitting out here all day? You look fried."

"What? No. Just a couple hours." I answered, realizing I forgot to put on sunscreen before I decided to sit outside. I've lived in two of the hottest states, and I still manage to forget sunscreen every time.

"That's my phone." He says, pointing to his phone in my hand, "Can I have it back?"

"Um yeah. Just a minute." I say, pulling the phone up to my ear, "Are you still there?"

"Smooth move, Wonder Woman." Roman says on the other line.

"Shut up, Robin." I roll my eyes, "I'm handing you to Batman."

Richard looks down on me with a confused expression, "Roman?"

"Yep." I wait for Richard's outstretched hand and place the phone gently in his palm, trying hard not to touch him.

"Don't go anywhere, let me talk to him real quick, but after I'd like to talk to you."

I feel the heat of my cheeks with the way my husband says he wants to talk to me. Richard always used to use regular phrasing when we'd talk around people, specifically at functions, but the phrases never meant what he said. He'd say he'd want to chat with me, and we'd

66

end up in the bathroom with him eating me out. He'd say he'd 'like to talk with me' and I'd find both of us naked under a pile of sheets. I couldn't really let that happen this time. The second Richard walked away from me, assumedly to put his shirt back on, I grabbed my mug and my book and booked it for the back entrance.

Chapter Ten

Amelia – Present

After a crazy day, I finally took up the guys' offer to take me out to the bar. Perhaps drinking and dancing is exactly what I need to get over my husband being in town. Since I learned that he'd be staying with my parents and working at the farm to help clean it up for the end of the season, I've been trying to keep my distance. The bar has been the furthest away from him I could get.

"I miss sex." Tanner sighs, "I miss being able to have a good night's worth of fun and not have to think about the repercussions the next day."

"Can we not talk about this in front of my sister?" Graves makes a distasteful click of his tongue before taking a large drink of his beer.

"I miss it too. Like frequently." I shoot my brother a grin, the face he makes just reminds me of the time he threw up when he walked in on me and Richard. I wince at the memory, realizing I won't have anyone to have public sex with, not even a quicky in a bedroom with an unlocked door.

"You two are bumming me out." My brother retorts, "That's why we're here." He waves his arm to the bar we're sitting at. This is anything but the kind of place I'd like to be in. Despite Tanner and Lucas telling me I needed to get out of my comfort zone and back into dating, this bar is not the place. This bar is filled with raggedy old men, some with holes in their shirts and shorts, some with a receding hairline but hair long enough it hangs past the barstool. I make a gagging sound before finishing my drink.

"This is not the place for that," Tanner says, just low enough for me to hear, "This is where we go to get your brother off our backs, and then we go to a club down the street." Tanner's smile is devious and it makes me chuckle.

"You're the devil."

"Your brother is the most *boring* old man we've ever met."

I burst out laughing as my brother shot us a look. We feign the look of innocence as if we weren't just talking about him.

"What's so funny?" My brother chides with a devilish look on his face, with his eyes focused on me and a smile just barely playing on his lips.

"Nothing." I say in answer.

"Just telling your sister about the time we beat your ass at billiards." Tanner covers his tracks better than I do, and I can't help but smile. I could definitely see Tanner being the kind of guy to have around for fun spontaneous dates. There's no telling what kind of girls he's into, but he definitely is the flirty and fun type, just based on what I've seen from him thus far.

"Is that your way of asking for a rematch?" Graves looks at him with a challenge glimmering in his eyes. There's a reason why Graves is called the Fox by his teammates, and it's not because of his looks, but by his cunning way of getting what he wants.

Graves is long gone by the time Tanner and I make it to this club he swears by. We're halfway to the bar when Lucas greets us, his flashy smile has charmed a swarm of girls at a nearby table. I've done my best to avoid alone time with these guys, knowing they're both extremely extroverted and seem to love the attention from women.

"Jersey chasers?" Tanner whispers to Lucas, who nods in answer.

"What?"

"They're girls who tend to flock to us because we're on a professional baseball team." Lucas answers, bending down to give me a quick side hug.

"Oh, the Florida team calls them cleat chasers." I say, biting my lip. The two of them nod.

"It's typical for this club. This is one of just two clubs that the team is allowed to come to—our drinks are comped and we're limited." Lucas rolls his eyes and smirks sheepishly, landing his hand on my shoulder.

"All because we're the best damn team in the states." Tanner adds, giving Lucas a high five.

I make a noise, "Are you sure about being the best?"

"This year was an exception." There's a glimmer in Tanner's eyes when he answers me.

I chuckle, "Relax. I don't actually care that much. I did. But I'm turning over a new leaf, no more worrying about baseball. In fact, tonight I want to drink and maybe hook up with a guy who knows nothing about sports."

"Don't shout that around here. You're in a club surrounded by guys who live off of baseball and football." Lucas' grin splits. "You guys want a drink, I'm gonna grab something real quick." We give him our drink of choice before he walks off.

I watch Tanner, who watches Lucas until he disappears, and when he turns back around, his cheeks redden. "You shouldn't be so picky. Sports guys are the best guys."

"Yeah? Do you know that from personal experience?" I ask with furrowed brows. I watch Tanner stumble over words, for only knowing him for a short time, I feel like I can read him very easily.

"Shit, girl. You're focusing on the wrong thing tonight." Tanner finally says.

I grin, "You're the one showing your cards."

"Shut up. Lucas doesn't know."

"He doesn't? Are you sure? Because to me, you're extremely..." I look for the right word to say, and instead of saying it, I use my hand, as I raise it and let it fall.

"Oh my god. Please don't tell Lucas." Tanner begs, "Your brother doesn't know either."

"I'm so confused on how they haven't put two and two together yet." I feel like Tanner's been extremely obvious since my first outing with him. I've noticed the way he looks at Lucas the most. If Tanner wasn't gay, I'd assume he was just gay for Lucas.

"Please don't say anything." Tanner begs again, giving me his puppy dog eyes.

"I don't plan to. I'm not that kind of girl." I pause, "Speaking of not that kind of girl, could you maybe be my wingman?"

"I'd be honored." Tanner answers with a grin just as Lucas appears with our drinks.

"Honored for what? Drinking the most alcohol?" Lucas jokes while nudging Tanner with his elbow. Tanner and I look at each other awkwardly before Tanner starts laughing, it sounds like a very fake laugh, but I don't question it.

"I asked Tanner to be my wingman tonight." I smile wickedly at Lucas to see if he has a reaction to Tanner helping me out.

"Oh." I watch Lucas look at Tanner for a brief moment before back at me, "He's good at that. I mean, with women, he knows what to say, don't you?" Lucas winks at him before his eyes scan back to me. "If he can't help you, I can."

Tanner shrugs, and gives me a quick look, "Let me see what I can do first."

The moment we leave the bar area, we're surrounded by loud music and loud people. I never had a reason to come to a club in the past, and the minute I told the guys I'd never been before, they said they'd make my first time memorable. We've been in limbo between the dance floor and the wall, where people are either making out or taking a drink break. Just when I was ready to ask one of them to dance with me, I turned around and saw neither of them at my side. Instead, they're chatting with two girls who lean against the wall. I feel my anxiety rise as I get ready to walk up to them, but I get pulled back, right at the moment where a server walks right in front of me.

"Hey!" I shout, just at the moment where I'm turned and find myself face to face with a good-looking man.

"Hey, sorry. I didn't mean to grab you like that. I just saw you almost collide with the server and her tray of drinks." The man yells back. I almost wince, but I wouldn't have heard him otherwise, so I just nod and give him a curt smile.

"Thanks." I shout back, I turn around and head to the only two people I know.

"Wait!" The guy shouts. I turned slowly, unsure if it was aimed at me. "Do you wanna dance?"

"You promise not to step on my toes?"

"Fancy heels ain't got nothing on my two step." He says with a smile.

"Lucky for you, I'm a boots girl." I point down to my shoes, showing off my low-cut cowboy boots.

"Never thought I'd see a country girl in a club." The guy says as we walk toward each other.

"Girl's gotta dance." I say with a small smile, as I put out my hand and let him take me out to the dance floor.

"What's your name, boots girl?" He asks as we find a small area and begin dancing like everyone around us.

"Amelia."

"Well, Amelia, I'm Kyle Ripley." It takes a minute for his name to settle in, the song stops just as a new one begins.

"Ripley? You've never by chance been to Evans Family Farm, have you?"

"I have actually. Twice, just during the summer—" He answered just as the bass dropped in the song. Neither of us heard much else, let alone spoke. We danced for three more songs before Kyle decided to get me a drink, I followed him to the bar to avoid being trampled by other dancers. He'd just handed me my drink when the DJ played a country song. It was rare for clubs in the city to play country, but then the DJ's voice took over the speakers.

"This is for all the locals, especially y'all wearing cowboy boots to a club."

I chuckled as I sucked the last of my drink and watched the number of people that left the dance floor and the ones that stayed and walked onto the floor with their boots.

"Shall we dance?" Kyle asked, offering his hand with a cute smile on his face.

I hesitated; country songs and line dances were always reserved for Richard, even before we were married, it was the one thing I could always expect from him. My husband was the perfect dance partner, the perfect man, never letting me walk onto the dance floor alone without him. The song playing wasn't ours, but from the same singer, and I was just supposed to accept a dance with a man not as handsome, but more considerate than my husband had been as of late...

Chapter Eleven

Amelia – Past

AMELIA (18), RICHARD (20)

"Have you seen Richard, Mrs. Greene?" I asked his mom the moment she opened the door. I watched her expression of greeting fall as she shook her head, I walked into their house the moment she opened the door more to let me in. I had been more considerate in the past, but I was in a rush and terribly upset. My prom had started two hours before, and I had waited for Richard to pick me up, but he never came. I ran to his room in hopes of finding him there, and he wasn't there. I groaned as I searched Richard's family house, his brother's room, and even his sisters' rooms. Thoughts of him breaking up with me salted my eyes, I knew better that Richard wouldn't do it on my prom night. The light that bounced off the windows in his family's house assaulted my eyes. The sun was no longer in the sky, just the remnants of the sunset that had yet to turn dark. The pink and purple cotton candy sky should've been a sign, there was never a sky so beautiful, not without rain. There was never a beautiful breeze without something to ruin it.

MIKA C.C.

I made it back home just long enough to throw off my scarf and had
every plan to slide my boots off, grab ice cream from the freezer, and
head to my bedroom. Instead, my peripheral vision noticed something
out of place on the hallway table. I dropped my purse and went for the
piece of paper on top of my parents key jar. I held up the piece of paper
as I read the words scribbled down.

> *You might be finding this late, but I wanted to make this night
> a little more memorable. Find me where we experienced our first
> cotton candy sunset. - RG*

I read aloud. I was going to kill him, Richard had really thought I'd
be okay with missing my prom for some silly scavenger hunt.

I didn't run, but I picked up my dress and walked briskly to the
place my boyfriend had made a riddle out of, I had every cuss word
ready to throw at him, every word that worked in place of 'jerk'. The
moment I'm halfway to the barn where Richard and I had our first
kiss, I see him leaning near the threshold for the horse's entrance.

"Richard!" I yell, preparing to give him our first fight. I watch his
comfortable stance change into a stiff one as he stands straight and
turns to face me.

He dares to smile at me as I approach him. I don't give him time to
even open his mouth when I'm finally in his space.

"Are you a dumbass? Do you really think I'd be okay with waiting
over two hours for you? Did you even bother to think of my feelings?
Are you that selfish? You really think spending a few minutes hooking
up in the barn would be enough for me? And you couldn't even be
bothered to wear a suit? I'm not taking you to my prom while you

wear jeans and a crummy t-shirt. What kind of girl do you take me for?" I get the last word out just as Richard bends down.

"What are you doing?" I breathe at the whiplash of my feelings as I watch him on one knee. "What do you think you're doing?"

"I was thinking of proposing to you, if you're done yelling, that is."

I take a sharp breath in, "*You're...* I'm done yelling." I say barely able to close my mouth, unable to believe this isn't more than just a daydream. Richard smiles slightly.

"Amelia, I love you. And I know I can be a '*dumbass*' sometimes, but I couldn't very well make your senior prom be as lame as mine. I had thought of a million different ideas for this night, and they all fell through within the last two hours, and for that, I'm sorry. I wanted to give you the best proposal ever. I want to be the best man for you, I want to give you everything, and that's why I can't go another moment without getting this ring on your finger." Richard takes a ring out of his pocket, it's not covered by a box, but it truly didn't need to be covered by a box when the gem shines in between his fingers.

"I also know this is the perfect ring because your mom told me so. I know this may come as a huge shock to you, but I have our lives planned out 'til we get old and gray, and if you don't want any of my plans, then I'll throw them to the wind and follow you wherever you go. I just want our lives to be perfect, and that starts with tonight. And I've already forgotten half of the speech I was trying to memorize, so I'm just going to say the thing." He pauses, not for effect but to swallow, I watch his throat bob and his hands shake.

Richard's nervous, something I'm not sure I've ever seen on him before. He's always been so confident during his baseball games, on dates with me, and the two times we've made love.

"Will you marry me, Amelia? Will you be my wife? Will you let me take you to prom as more than just my girlfriend?"

I feel the first tears fall down my cheeks, "Yes. Yes, you dumbass. Yes, a million times." I answered all three questions with a sob and grin on my face.

I watch Richard slide the ring on my finger as I notice his hands are no longer shaking. He stands up so fast that I forget about our height difference, it doesn't matter when he pulls me up, his arms underneath my bum as my hands hold onto his face, our lips meet and I feel him spin us once as we kiss. I smile in between kisses as he helps my feet find the ground, I feel his hands slide up my silk dress as I pull him to me to kiss me again. Richard may have to stoop down for me to kiss him, but I don't care, especially when I'm not ready to stop kissing him. I want to hold onto the feeling of being his forever.

Not an hour later, and I'm walking into my senior prom with a gorgeous princess-cut opal gemstone on my ring finger, engaged. Both my parents and Richard's had known his plans and were waiting and watching from the back porch of my family's house. My dad took a million pictures of us right after Richard changed into his suit he had hid in my brother's closet. Apparently he had it there regardless of where the engagement would've happened, since he knew we'd tell my parents the news first.

My mom had cried while my dad explained that my boyfriend had asked for his permission, only three months after we started dating and continued asking the same question every few months for con-firmation. Richard's mother was ecstatic for us, giving us praises that went well with her big bear hugs. His mom was truly the definition of my second mother, mother-in-law didn't even come close to the feelings I had for her as his mother. The moment Richard Sr. agreed to take our first family photo together was the moment I knew I was marrying into the right family. There was no mistake, no adolescent thought that passed when I knew: I loved Richard and his family, and they loved me right back.

My senior prom was one of the best nights of my life. Between Richard's proposal and a bit of time with our parents, by the time we made it to the prom, there was maybe an hour left. That was the first time I followed Richard's plans, and it had been the perfect night. We had still gotten to dance to our favorite song, we still got to line dance to the cheesy songs that played, we even got to tell my classmates about our engagement. It was the first night the cotton candy sky didn't follow up with a bad memory.

Chapter Twelve

Richard – Present

I had spent half an hour at the pub watching my wife drink with her roommate and brother, I had spent another half hour sitting in the car watching the three of them eat fast food before they dropped her brother off. I had been in stalker mode the moment I found her in that bar, I had only gone to have one or two drinks, but the moment I saw my wife, I stopped drinking. I'd never been one to party, no matter how many parties I'd been invited to, even when my teammates would practically tour the clubs in every state we played in, I never stuck around to get drunk with them. Only a few of my teammates knew my thoughts on drinking. My dad hadn't been a drinker, but it only took once to know that he was a violent drunk. And it only took once, when my youngest sibling was only a few months old, for the whole family to experience one bad memory of him stumbling in, yelling and smacking our mother across the face. That one experience had changed our lives, our dad never touched a drink after seeing the expressions on his kids faces, all of us grew up never touching hard liquor, nor did we have over 2 beers. We'd been scarred for life, but the moment I saw my wife dancing with another man, it was a whole new version of scarring.

I wasn't drunk, but the moment I stepped onto that dance floor, I felt my body shift, an almost dizzying feeling. I might not have been drunk on liquor, but I was drunk on jealousy, drunk on lust for my wife. She looked so fucking beautiful in a dress that I know she'd never wear at any public event with me on her arm. All this over the little pink dress that crept up her thighs the more she danced, that showed too much cleavage for this asshole to stare at for four fucking songs. The second Amelia was about to take this man's hand to line dance was the moment I stepped in, I wouldn't let her go this far. I wouldn't let him take advantage of my wife.

"Can I have this dance?" I said as the country song began.

Amelia whipped her head towards me, with the curls in her hair bouncing. "Richard?" She looked back at the man with an exasperated expression on her face before she faced me.

"Amelia." I cooed with my hand open for her to take. Her reluctant hand waited in the air, unsure of who's hand to take.

"What are you doing here?" She tried to whisper-yell the question but definitely landed as more of a holler.

"Dance with me, and maybe I'll tell you." I answered, getting even closer to her body to cover her from the creep.

Amelia looked up at me with a gleam in her eyes, either I had just saved her from the guy or she was pissed, which I knew was the possibility that she was actually both. But once our eyes met, I knew who she'd chosen to dance with. Amelia looked back at him and excused herself, as she took my hand and quickly walked me to the dance floor, versus me leading her.

MIKA C.C.

The moment our feet hit the linoleum dance floor, we moved like nothing had changed. Our dance moves, our hands entwined, her breaths falling into rhythm with the music, just as mine had done the same. We were still the same people, at least when it came to dancing...

"Why are you here, Richard? Are you following me?" I gulped, knowing I couldn't very well tell her someone had to keep a safe eye on her.

"I came here to dance with my wife, no other intentions than that."

"No other intentions?" One of Amelia's brows raised in question. "And here I was thinking you had the intention of doing something crazy like punching the guy I was with."

"I would, I still could." I said in between breaks of the song.

"Richard."

"I won't." I pause as our feet meet together just to step two feet back and meet again. "What will it take to get you to forget the dancing monkey?"

"I didn't come with him."

"Well, of course you didn't. Your roommates are having a good time of their own." I smirked as I pointed with my chin to the gay guy and the other one. She looks, seeing what I see, the one making out with a girl and the other drinking a beer while doing the two-step dance too far away from the girl who's supposed to be his dancing partner.

"He loves him." She says as her hair nearly whips my face as she turns back to face me.

"Is that right?" I ask, feigning interest.

"The other doesn't know it yet though."

"Isn't that how it always goes?" I question her, watching the corners of her mouth turn down after just being in a closed-lipped smile.

"What do you mean?" I watch the strobe light colors shine through her eyes. Her piqued curiosity has me planning my next move as my hand moves at the back of her neck, moving her hair out of the way so I can feel the pulse of her heart under her soft skin. The way her body conforms to my hands on her. Amelia doesn't move, not when she knows I can feel her heart beating fast and not from the dancing. I can smell her perfume mixed with her musk, and if I weren't a gentleman, I'd be kissing her already. The moment her eyes dip down to my lips is when I stop us from swaying to the song. I licked my lips previously, but they feel rough the moment my lips meet with her soft lips. Amelia's arms drape down her body, it's the first time I've never had her hands on me in our entire relationship of kisses. I lick her lips with hopes that it makes her grip onto me but nothing I do does it, not until my tongue enters her mouth and I taste the alcohol on her. Not until her tongue slams back into my mouth that her arms wrap around me like she used to. I'd make out with her on every dance floor of every club if it meant she understood that I live for her touch and her mouth on mine.

Amelia pulls her lips off of me for separating us with her hand on my chest, "Richard." She says my name through deep breaths in the same way I used to make her moan my name. I bring her lips back to mine, but as quickly as we meet, Amelia stops me from going further.

"No, Richard." I pull back from her, knowing that my wife stands on business. Amelia never says anything she doesn't mean. "What the fuck are you trying to do to me?"

"What? Nothing."

"You seduced me. You're trying to get me back, and you think that I'm just going to come back to this version of you by doing what? By acting like your old self?"

"Amelia, I—"

"Dammit, Ramsey, I almost fucking fell for it. I'm so stupid." I watch her shake her head at me.

"I'm not trying to do anything—" I start untangling my hand from between her hair and neck, letting my hand rest on her shoulder.

"Leave me alone, Ramsey." Amelia pushes me off her, my hands fall at my sides as I watch her walk off the dance floor and walk out with her two roommates by her side. As I stand there, still amongst the swaying dancers and upbeat music.

Amelia - Present

"So are we going to talk about the hottie from the club?" Tanner asks as he slides into the dining room nook. The entire table and benches were built by my grandfather, I'm not surprised that everything is still in amazing condition, though I'm surprised that these three haven't trashed everything. Of course, I pretend I didn't hear him as I eat my cereal and stare at my phone as my favorite show lights up the screen.

"I can be *really* talkative if you don't answer me." Tanner threatens, but I continue to avoid the conversation. It's been two measly days since I was almost ravaged on the dance floor by my own husband. "Hey Graves, did we tell you about your sister at the club?"

I roll my eyes knowing this man is fucking with me, I don't bite when it comes to blackmail, especially when a person is bluffing.

"No, what happened?" My brother's voice comes from behind me. I stiffen and look at Tanner. He's definitely not bluffing now. I swallow my bite of cereal as Tanner challenges me with his eyes.

I turn to look at Graves, "Tanner and I got to do an Eiffel Tower with some random guy, right in the club bathroom."

Graves' face falls, "Please tell me you're kidding?"

I look back at Tanner and watch his face turn pale, I've never seen a man look so scared. I'm sure Tanner is aware of Graves' anger issues, so I have no doubt Tanner is trying to figure out how to not look like an asshole in front of my brother.

"I am kidding." I answer with a quick smirk. Graves' brows furrow as he looks at me.

"Why? Why are you so disgusting?"

I shrug as I get up from my seat, grabbing my empty bowl, "Listen, you need to loosen up, and if anyone were to do it, wouldn't you want it to be your sister?" I pat Graves' shoulder and walk past him to put my dishes in the sink.

"Usually guys only loosen up by fucking someone, and you know your brother better than anyone. He's got a stick shoved so far up his ass he doesn't even realize when a girl likes him." Tanner says bluntly. It causes both me and my brother's heads to look at Tanner as he sips his coffee.

"Did he just –?" I ask Graves.

"He sure did." My brother answers quickly with a surprised look on his face, something that doesn't happen often enough to my brother.

"Are you going to kick his ass?" My genuine question has me looking attentively at Graves.

"I don't think I will." My brother shrugs as he frowns slightly, taking a sip of his own coffee. He walks off, not even bothering with a response to Tanner. I'm simply in awe as I watch Graves walk to his room without another word. I nearly miss the chair when I go to sit back down across from Tanner.

"I'm sorry, how did you just go from ghost boy to this?" I ask with my mouth still agape from my brother's response.

Tanner sets his mug down and sighs, "I don't fucking know. I don't even know if that was really me." He actually sounds scared as he says his words, "Am I going to be brutally murdered in my sleep?"

I laugh, "What the hell, Tanner? Do you have a personality disorder you don't know about?"

"I just sometimes let my thoughts come out of my mouth, but I've never said them in front of Graves before." Tanner frowns, "Seriously though, is he?"

I chuckle and shake my head, "You would've been dead already."

"Kind of like how you'd be if I had told him about you and mystery boy?" Tanner's brows rise in question.

I roll my eyes, "Wow, you may *actually* be good at manipulation."

"Of course I am, Amelia. I do it for a living, how many pitchers do you know that aren't good at manipulation?" He says with a smirk, "Though, I still am scared shitless of your brother despite that."

I giggle, "You're not gonna let go of the club guy thing, until I tell you?"

Tanner's lips purse together, "Pretty much. Plus, you have some-thing on me, so it seems right to have this on you."

I feign a scoff, "You're a horrible friend."

"I know." He shrugs. "Now give me all the dirty details."

After I check to make sure no one will hear us, I tell Tanner. I told Tanner everything.

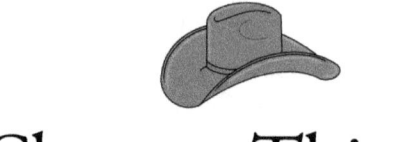

Chapter Thirteen

Amelia – Present

I should've known my dad's truck would break down on the way to his house, the signs were there, and I completely avoided them as I pulled into my parents driveway. I just barely paid attention to my surroundings as I had walked into my parents house, greeting their dog first and then walking to the kitchen to check on my mom's plants. It took all of five minutes to care for them and the dog until I turned and audibly yelled at the man who had barely made it a foot through the front door's threshold. The thunder in the sky added to his arrival. The dog reacted as if Richard was an old friend, wagging his tail for him like he was his actual owner.

"What are you doing here?" Richard asked with a brow raised, as he closed the door behind him.

I answered with a heave, "My mom asked me to take care of the plants. I thought you weren't staying here anymore?"

"I changed my mind." He shrugs, shooting a look quickly at me before he looks elsewhere. I don't bother following his gaze as I turn back towards the plants and count them to make sure I've watered each of them.

"Right." I swallow, feeling a bit nervous since the last time I saw him. Being alone with my husband shouldn't be something to be worried about, but between the last words I said to him and being alone with him makes me want one of two things to happen. The first, for Richard to leave and never bother me again, or the second, for him to somehow show me that he's here for me and not just to make things right between us, but actually do something besides what he's done in the past. I'd been hoping for the latter since he's staying at my parents house while they're out of town.

"Amelia—" Richard starts. As soon as he says my name, it sounds like he's going to say something life-changing, and I'm not sure I can deal with it. His voice sounds too sad, his eyes scream for me to look at him, but I'm too afraid. Afraid of the rejection, afraid of the aftermath. There's a reason why I left after I told him how I felt, and it's this...

"I should get going." I say as I pass him and open the door, not only to the sound of heavy rain, but also to the water gushing from the roof of my parents house. I should've questioned why they didn't have rain gutters, but it was California, so I couldn't blame them completely.

"Let me drive you."

"You really don't have to drive me back to the farmhouse." I said with a wipe of my chin. It'd been so long since we'd gotten a good storm. Now that the rain was pouring, all I had wanted was to enjoy the rain, even if that meant walking over half an hour from house to house. I knew the area wasn't bad, and the rain virtually wiped out any wild animals from looking for prey.

"Not sure I'm okay with you walking back." Richard says as he starts up my brother's truck. He clicks his tongue as it takes a minute for it to start up.

I roll my eyes at him as he makes another noise and backs out of the driveway. I want to snap at him, but I stop myself from doing so, as I look at him as his arm stretches over the back of my seat, as he looks out the back window. Richard looks different, I don't know if it's because I've told him the worst part of me, or because he knows he fucked up, either way, I can't fully read his expression without feeling a little guilty.

By the time he turns back around and starts driving down the dirt road back to the ranch, I start to notice it. I finally noticed what he said. Richard did say he wasn't the man he used to be, I know it had been hard for him to admit who he'd been over the last year, but now he was changing. Not reverting back to who he was, but learning... He stopped the car suddenly just as a group of teens rode their dirt bikes over the road, I didn't notice it until I looked down and found his arm outstretched again, this time over my chest as protection. I wanted to thank him, but there was something holding me back, there always has been lately.

Once Richard picked back up driving, I thought we'd make it back even faster than normal. The rain had managed to stop as I looked out the window to the horse's stables and our chicken coop. We had just passed the beginning of my family's farm, when I looked hard enough at the farm to notice a horse out of the stable, with his leg stuck in between the fence and gate.

"Richard!" I pat his shoulder urgently, "Pull over. Pull over right now!" I barely wait until he has the truck in park that I open the door and bolt. I hear him yell my name, but I don't bother listening to him to slow down. I've run down slopes of grass before, but my feet keep me humble as I stumble slightly and fall, just to roll down the wet grass. Ramsey barely makes his way to me, before I get up and jump the fence. I hear my husband yell at me again, but his voice is almost drowned out by the horse's constant whines. I make it to the horse just in time, she's in pain and keeps trying to pull, but it doesn't seem to help her.

"Amelia, are you insane? You could've been hurt!" Richard says as he stomps over to me.

I grumble under my breath as I try to figure out the best way to get the horse free.

"Let me see your shoulder." He says, coming up on me like I haven't been able to handle my own injuries by myself.

"No." I push him away, "It doesn't even hurt, there are bigger problems here."

"The horse?! Amelia, your life is way more important than the animals right now."

"I get that! But the horse is hurt, and I am fine, Richard! Now if you could just shut up and help me get her free, then we can go back to not talking to each other." I turn away from him and focus back on the horse. I wish my brother had bothered to name these horses, as I know it's easier to calm them down with soft words and a gentle touch. His not giving the horse a name makes me feel disconnected from the creature. Richard seemed to shut up as I tried a technique I used to do to help the chicken's feet free off the barbed wire. The technique didn't work, and as soon as I put my hand back on the horse's foot, it pulled, causing me to fall back. Richard picks me back up, just in time for the rain to start again.

"Of course." He grumbles out loud.

"She can feel your anger, Richard."

"She can't feel yours?" He bites back.

I stand to look him in the eyes, "Do you really want to fight right now? In the rain, with a horse that needs attention?"

"And what if I did, Amelia? What would be so wrong with fighting? Why is it so hard for you to let me fight for you?"

"I have no fight left! I've said everything I needed to, Richard. I'm just trying to get over you, and it starts with helping this horse." I turn back around and go back to helping the horse.

I hear both Richard and the horse huff at me, like I'm the problem; they both have such an attitude towards me. I groan as I try to pull the horse free, and it doesn't work.

"Alright, enough. Let me try." Richard says as he bends down to work on getting the horse free. I watch as his hand reaches up to the horse's thigh and rubs it.

"It's gonna be okay, girl, I've got you." Richard whispers before he brings his hand back down and puts his hands between the bottom of the gate and fence. He doesn't even hesitate when his hand slips under the rain, his hand goes right back and separates the gate from the fence. His strength supersedes mine as his light touch helps move the horse's foot from the spot. I whisper under my breath about him always being the horse whisperer.

The horse neighs and runs away. I almost go after her, but I watch her run freely with no limp or any sort of problems, not as she makes it under the stables. The rain lets up a bit, a slight drizzle just coating us, though I know I'm soaked. The clouds start to pass, leaving us in the wake of a dusk sky.

"What a crazy storm." I say as I look up at the stars just starting to peek through the night sky, "Always so beautiful after." There's a silence, a long and heavy one, one I can't help but try and fill, but right as I'm about to, I feel a hole burning in the side of my head.

"Beautiful is an understatement." Richard cuts the silence. I look back at him, staring at me. "Amelia, can I please talk to you?"

I quickly look away, already feeling tears prickling my eyes, "We should head back before it gets any darker out." I don't let him ask me another thing as I start walking up the slight hill back to the truck.

Richard follows, slowly but steadily, as we make it to the truck. Both of us look at the wheels, stuck and settled into mud.

"Well shit." I start to say, ready to tell Richard to begin walking.

"Easy fix. I'll get the truck out, no problem." He says, before bolting himself into the truck. I keep a fast pace to keep up with him.

"You're not going to be able to get it out of the mud, it's —"

"Amelia, I can get this truck out of the mud. I know how to do this kind of thing."

I fold my arms at his words and back away, "Sure. Of course, because all men know everything." I roll my eyes and keep my mouth closed, I even take an extra step back.

Richard starts the truck and begins to press on the gas. The tires spin and get deeper into the mud. He sighs, and I assume he puts the car in reverse, because when he hits the gas again, the tires spin even faster and mud goes everywhere. I gasp and scream as mud gets on me.

"Richard!" I yell. He looks over at me and holds in his smile. He turns off the car and gets out, first looking at the damage and then looking at me.

"Yeah, I guess we're gonna be spending the night in the bed of the truck."

"I'd rather walk home."

"No, the hell you won't. It's dark and there's mountain lions, coyotes and foxes out here." Richard nearly yells at me.

I sigh, "I don't really want to be stuck out here with you and the night sky right now." I start to walk away, but he grabs for my arm and spins me around.

"What's so bad about spending a night with me, huh? What's so bad about talking to me? You used to love it. You used to love me, remember?"

"Richard... I-I don't know where to start."

"You don't have to, let me. Let me tell you everything I need to tell you."

I look at him, "What if I don't like what you have to say?"

"When have you ever not liked what I had to say? Whenever this doubt started is when you started hiding this stuff from me, and if I'd known... Well, you know exactly what I would've done to fix it."

"It might've gotten worse last year, but you and I both know our relationship wasn't where we wanted it to be for the last ten years."

"I know, and if I could go back in time and fix the last ten years for us, I would. All I want to do now is prove to you that you've always been *my* center of gravity, my light and my *everything*." His fingertips ghost over my skin as if he's unsure if he should touch me.

"And what if I don't react the way you expect me to?"

94

"Then I'll throw you over my shoulder and show you exactly what I missed doing to you." The smile that crept up on Richard's face said enough, but I still couldn't give into him, no matter how much that expression had a hold on me.

"I appreciate that you're so willing to mend this."

"Are you?"

"Am I what?" The question seemed to simply hang in the air between us, thick and sweaty air, the type that had me ready to either run away from him or run right back into his arms.

"Appreciative. Are you truly appreciative of me?" The birds and bugs around us seemed to stop chirping and buzzing, almost as if they were waiting for my answer, too.

"Richard, I don't know what you want me to say. If I say yes, then what?"

"Then, this." He says as he pulls my ponytail, forcing my head up, his lips hover over mine for a nanosecond before they meet in a searing kiss. My entire body feels like it's on fire from his hold on my hair, I hadn't even noticed he had wrapped his hand around my hair. I hadn't noticed how quickly he towered over me, our lips together can only mean one thing to him, especially when I don't push him away fast enough. Richard is so attentive when it comes to turning me on that I've almost forgotten why I left him to begin with.

I feel the vibration of my lips against his, unsure of which one of us is moaning as our lips spread apart for our tongues to meet. I can't remember the last time our tongues met like this, ever since we'd been married, it's always been pecks of kisses, even when having sex, it's always been lips, never tongue. I find myself lost in the moment when my hands find the back of his arms and I try to pull him closer. The only way we could get closer is if we were naked and in my room. Our tongues circle in each other's mouths, and it's not until I feel his tongue lick the roof of my mouth, that I shudder and nearly giggle. It's my smile that breaks our lips apart, and Richard backs away, though I don't let him get far with my hands still holding onto him. My smile falls when he looks at me like he's a lost puppy.

"I can't be me without you, Amelia." He says pushing my wet hair behind my ear.

"And I can't be me when I'm with you, Richard."

"How can I change that? I need you more than I need—" His words cut off, and I see the sorrow behind his eyes.

"More than you need, what?"

Richard shakes his head, "There's nothing I need. There's nothing that's essential to my life, not when you're not in it."

I groan because it's those words that make me pull his shirt, him, back to me, back to his lips on mine.

"Fuck." He mutters, as my hands tangle in his hair, as he pulls me up, up onto the bed of the truck.

This time I mutter the same words as I feel his hand dip under the elastic of my shorts. I want to scream, I want to forget everything about our past and start all over. Fuck it if it means I can have him like the man he is right now, with his fingers having no problem finding my slit and filling my pussy.

"Richard–" I whisper-moan. He shushes me with his lips back on mine.

"It's only us out here, and there's only one thing I want to do to show you how much I've missed you."

One of my eyebrows raises in question, "Only one thing?"

"Lie back for me, Ames." He looks at me with a criminal stare, one I only know as what he's about to do might be illegal. We're stuck in the mud anyways, and I know if I don't lay back, Richard's fingers deep inside me will make me want to. I lay back only slightly, with my fat folding in as I look at him.

"What are you planning?" I ask knowing that it's one of two things. I don't have a chance to question him any further when he shuts me up with a blinding kiss. Our tongues dance as I feel him push me down further and bite my bottom lip as he pulls himself off me.

"Stay down for me, baby." Richard says with a glimmer in his eye, as his free hand pushes my chest back before he dives into my neck, kissing my sensitive skin. I stifle a moan as the fingers still hook inside me. He works his way down, kissing my breasts through my t-shirt, finding my nipples and nibbling at them. My hair untangles from the elastic as he sheds the shirt off of me.

I fight the urge to call out his name again, trying to remind myself that what he's doing is good, and that I don't need to be self-conscious over the body he's seen a million times. It's when Richard gets down to my shorts that he pulls them off, and I'm holding onto my stomach, trying to hide the folds that are on display. He swats my hand away.

"What are you doing, trying to hide yourself from me?" Richard asks in a whisper as I try to cover myself again. He pulls my hand away and interlocks our fingers together to stop me from doing it again.

"Hiding my rolls, my fat." I say plainly. It makes him pause and pull his fingers out of me. I feel empty without him.

He comes up to look me in the eyes, "Oh baby, you're nowhere close to fat. Even if you were, you'd look just as beautiful as you do now. As you always have."

"It's not attractive." I say, trying to look away from him.

Richard pulls my chin to look at him, "You are the most attractive woman I've ever laid eyes on." I refuse to believe it even as he looks at me with stars in his eyes.

"I'm sure that's true." I say sarcastically. Right then I feel him grab my chubby waist.

"These?"

I let out a noise.

"You call it fat or your chub. I call it *perfect* for me to grab onto. These love handles are meant for me to pull you to me and show you exactly how perfectly you fit in my arms."

I gulp at his words.

"These." He says again, this time holding onto my back fat. "Your back rolls? They're not rolls. It's the perfect area for my fingers to sink into you, especially when I'm fucking you from behind."

"Richard," I say in a half-moan, half-sob.

"This." In finality, he grabs my stomach, the area that hangs. "This held our world. This has the opportunity to grow a human, one that we can make together."

"Please." I feel tears ready to fall from my eyes if they haven't already, "Why are you doing this?"

"Because you are not fat. You are perfect. You are perfect for me, no matter what size you wear, no matter if your belly is big or not. You are the only woman I want to see naked every night."

I can taste my tears now, "Oh, god. Richard." I pull him to me and kiss him hard. Our lips, our tongues meeting, our hands entangling together, as I lay in the bed of the truck with me naked. I want to cover myself up with him, but just as I think we've finished whatever this is, Richard goes back down.

"I have every intention of still showing you how much you mean to me. How much I've missed you. How much I fucking love you." I feel tears spill after every sentence he speaks, and then I feel his tongue swirl around my clit. I moan and sob around him, while he licks my pussy all over, sucking on my lips and teething my clit slightly. His fingers re-enter me, and I call out his name when his fingers hit my g-spot just as his tongue circled my clit again and again.

My legs clench around his head as my hands go straight into his hair, my fingers wrapping in his thick hair, until I can feel his scalp. Richard moans as he moves his face further into my pussy, his tongue moving endlessly with his fingers deep inside me. He's made me orgasm time and time again, but this time I'm aware of where his free hand roamed, how he gripped my stomach, and how he held me down by my love handles.

Richard was right, his hand does fit perfectly on me. Just the thought of that with the feel of what he's doing to me causes my toes to curl as I feel myself cum against his tongue. Richard laps and sucks every bit of my orgasm up, and I'm left panting and sweating in the California heat. When he comes up to look at me, I assume he sees my mascara down my face. But the expression on Richard's face says otherwise, not when I see his lips upturn, with my arousal almost dripping from his chin, as he shows his perfect smile at me.

"God, I love looking at you." Richard says before placing a peck on my lips, the kiss almost doesn't register in my brain, not when he dips his head again and lets me taste myself against his tongue. I moan,

I've never thought I tasted good before, but then again, I used to be adamant about not letting him kiss me after he's gone down on me.

"You hear me, Amelia? I fucking love you." He says in between our kisses.

"Stop talking." I say as I pull him back down onto my lips.

Richard - Present

I pull my pants down just far enough to expose my hard cock to Amelia, I hadn't planned on fucking her, but the minute I tasted her against my lips and my tongue, I wanted more. Amelia had to have known my problems with fucking her, but since the barn, I felt like a new man. Maybe it had been the change of scenery or the fact that both of us had bared our souls to each other... Whatever it had been, had brought that part of me back to life.

"Fuck, Rich." Amelia hummed as I pushed my cock slowly inside her pink, swollen pussy.

I click my tongue, "You. Are. Mine." I say as I pump my cock into her a bit more. I can feel her fingernails digging into my skin even with my long-sleeve on, the shirt hadn't been mine for long, but I felt the material tighten as I gripped my wife more to fuck her.

"Yeah?" She dared to moan back.

"Yes, Amelia. You. Are. Mine. And I. Am. Yours." I answer, filling her up with my cock. My wife moans again as I draw myself out just to push right back in, the buildup between us has been too much. Between fucking her in the barn and now, I've had to take my time getting her to open up to me. I need to make Amelia understand that there is no one else and that no matter what she looks like, she will always come first. I've done a shit job at showing her, but that's the past. I have to prove to her that from now on, I won't be a shitty husband.

Amelia's eyes roll back as her grip tightens. "Please," Her grasp is needy; her voice craves for more. I know what she wants—what she's begging for as she pleads for me again. The urge to fuck her with my tongue strikes me with a force as her body jolts with pleasure. I look down at Amelia as her eyes roll back and drops of water fall on her, I glance up to make sure it's not my sweat but a shower of rain, not heavy enough to get me to stop, as I continue to fuck her.

I grip her waist, her perfect body molding into my palms as I fuck her harder and faster, knowing if I fucked her with my tongue again I wouldn't be able to come inside her. Amelia's body contracts into me, her pelvis thrusting harder into me as my cock barely juts out of her just to slide back into her wet cunt. Amelia screams just as a round of heat lightning bolts above us, the perfect sight to behold as she comes around my cock. I can't stop, not until I'm coming deep inside of her, not until I've shown her I mean business when I say she is mine.

"Richard." She says between hitched breaths, her body still reacting, still sensitive from her orgasm. My dick thrusting inside her until I feel myself reach the release. "Oh my god!" she shouts as I feel myself come around her as her legs tighten around me. I slowly pump in her as she looks up at me. The expression on Amelia's face speaks volumes, it says more than I think she realizes. Every time I begin a sentence with her name, she stops me, so this time I don't.

"I love you, Turtle." Amelia's eyes water at my sentence, her chest heaving, her body still holding onto me after what just happened. Her hands reach my face as she pulls me down to her lips. The kiss is rough, hard, and needy. Her tongue pushes against my lips just enough for me to give her mine in what I thought would be something quick. Our tongues and lips turn hungrier, as my cock begins to harden inside of her. Amelia moans at the feel of me filling her up again, as her pelvis thrusts against me. I can't tell if she's trying to tell me she loves me too or if this is just a thank you for telling her how I felt. I'd take whatever I can get from my wife, but the thought of her not saying she loves me back plagues my thoughts. The thought of my wife not loving me anymore fucks me up, but I can't stop, I can't stop trying to win her back. I would fuck her like this every day if it meant she'd tell me she loves me.

We'd spent the night fucking each other in her dad's truck, if my mind had been right, I would've never taken her back to the farmhouse. But when morning came, we rode in silence all the way there. I had planned to kiss her goodbye, with the hopes that the kiss would prove that I'm here and hers. The moment I walked her up the stairs to the door, was the moment I froze up. I'd never froze during a game, never froze up at any point in our relationship. The thought of the night before and the three words I had said danced around in my head. I had let her in, but the moment we were on the front porch, with me reliving the night before, was when I realized she still hadn't. Amelia still hadn't let down her walls, she might've let me fuck her and kiss her like we loved each other, but there was something missing. There had to have been. Why wouldn't she say it back? Why would she let me make love to her all night if she didn't feel it?

"I'll see you later?" were the words Amelia said to me before I let her walk in the farmhouse without some sort of answer to last night, without touching her like I had last night. I had simply nodded my head and watched her hips sway as she entered the house with the door closing behind her softly.

I had either severely fucked up or needed to prove to her that this was not going to be a two-time thing. I could only imagine Amelia would either hate me for it or love me for it, but I was left with barely any options. Winning my wife back wasn't an easy task, but the challenge was worth it.

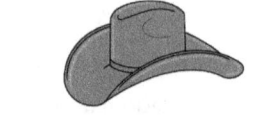

Chapter Fourteen

Amelia – Present

Avoiding Richard had become my hobby, my sport and my career all at once. In Florida he'd been like a ghost, but of course in California he'd been a living, breathing person, invading my space at every chance he had. The days I spent not around Richard had felt faster; maybe I had put myself to work to avoid my thoughts of what was to come, and the thoughts of him here didn't put my mind at ease either. Ever since Tanner and Luke had put me to work, I'd spent a good portion of my time not having to bother or worry about Richard finding me. Maybe it'd been silly, but even at the gym I felt like Richard was watching me. When I went to therapy, I had moments where I imagined him hearing everything I said. I was being haunted by my husband, and it wasn't even the real him. I had visited my parents less, but they came over more to the farmhouse, with Richard staying in my parents house. I thought I'd be safe with him there and me here, but I was wrong. My parents, no matter their age, had put Richard to work. Even though both of my parents had retired from their life on the farm, both still had taken care of things since Graves and his roommates didn't always have the time. Now they had put Richard to do all of it. Now I had to deal with seeing him when I was taking care of the animals in the morning...

I had spent most of my mornings on the farm, feeding the chickens, cleaning their coop and then spending some much-needed time with the horses. Even though the horses were tamed, I knew my brother didn't interact with them too much; the little time I had spent with them had told me they weren't used to the interactions. One of the horses, an American paint horse, seemed to be spooked by my sudden movements, but I couldn't help but try and train both myself and the horse to get over that fear. She reminded me a bit of Callie with the way she'd slowly walk away from people, but this horse was different. Even for myself, I knew getting too close could cause the horse to rear. I caught myself letting this one come to me. I named the mare Mocha just from the brown and white spots all over her body, but she never seemed to answer to the nickname.

"Donna." Richard's voice called from outside the stables, and I continued to brush Mocha's mane as she neighed. He called the name again, and Mocha shook my hands off her. I backed up expecting her to begin rearing; instead, she started for a quick pace out of the stables. I peeked, not wanting Richard to know where I was, as I watched the horse go right up to Richard, his hands wrapped around her chin and muzzle.

"Horse whisperer." I said to no one but myself. I rolled my eyes as I looked over at the Friesan horse I had named Shadow, who had

105

just lurked enough into the stables. His nostrils flared as he sniffed the riding gear, giving me an idea. I smirked. "Let's take a ride, Shadow."

I hadn't waited much longer—well, just long enough for Richard to get distracted by his phone while Mocha, or Donna, as he called the horse, roamed freely. I had just mounted the horse when I looked down at my phone ringing; it brightened in the dark stable. Richard's name shining bright on my phone with a picture of us kissing in the background. The sound of my phone caused my heart to stir, especially with the crunches of Richard's shoes coming closer to the stables. I quickly tapped the side of my foot on the stallion to start it's trollop, but with an accidental tap, Shadow picked up his pace.

"Whoa." My voice croaked out, and as I grabbed the reins, Shadow sprinted past Richard. Richard's head whipped to watch as my hair bounced in the wind. I looked back just enough to see him getting smaller by the minute.

Shadow neighed as she bolted around the property. With one hand tight on the horn of the saddle, I pet the horse, letting him know he could slow down. Even with the light taps of my feet, Shadow didn't feel the need to slow down. My head dizzied as the stallion ran the length of the ranch, and my stomach curled with just coffee in my system. I didn't realize how long it'd been since I ate, how long it had been since I rode a horse last, almost a decade. Shadow was an experienced horse, one that was made for riding and competition, perhaps he had been used as a competitive horse before my brother had brought it onto the farm. Either way, the stallion was not done showing me his fast movements.

I was barely halfway back to the stables when the horse that betrayed me showed up with their accomplice on her back. Richard held his wide-brimmed hat in place as the horses just barely passed each other. I looked back just long enough to see Mocha-Donna turn around. I huffed as Shadow's legs finally started to slow. Richard and the horse caught up to us just in time. I kept my head straight, trying hard not to give my husband any ideas, though the vision from my periphery watched him as he tried hard to get his horse to keep up with Shadow.

"Does this horse have your personality or what?" Richard chided with a snicker. I shook my head in response, looking the opposite way, hoping he'd get the hint. I felt my rein tug from my hand just long enough to look and see Richard wrapping both mine and his reins into a knot.

"What do you think you're doing? Untie that right now!" I say trying to reach over to grab the reins. Richard's hand pulls the reins, pulling Shadow closer to the mare. The two horses sigh and groan. I relate as I feel my balance teeter, as I feel a hand wrap around my waist and part of my ass to keep me from falling over. I look at Richard's hand and follow the movement he makes when he removes his hand from me.

"Sorry." He says with a gulp. Apparently my husband feeling me up makes both of us nervous as I feel my stomach flip as I watch his Adam's apple bob up and down.

"Me too." I say as I look away from him. Unsure exactly what I'm sorry for, but it needed to be said regardless. The sound of the world around us seems to fill the awkward silence, along with the constant noises from the horses as they walk close together.

"I miss you." Richard's words catch me off guard as I look and lean just to glare at my husband. My body losing its balance in the process.

I grab for the horn, but my foot slips out of the stirrup, causing my body to fall further while kicking Mocha-Donna in the stomach. Both the horse and I yelp as half my body leans off of Shadow. I close my eyes, expecting to fall further with the horses being tied together, but whatever Richard does above me gets the horses to stop suddenly. I let go of the horn just to fall into the grass and get back up, except I don't feel the sting of the sharp grass, just a hard surface under me. I look up to see Richard looking down at me.

"What—How? You caught me?" I ask, feeling his muscles flex under me.

"You think I'd ever let you fall?" His brows crease. "Are you okay?"

"Just lost my balance. I'm not sure I needed a super-cowboy to save me." I answered, flicking the top of his cowboy hat.

"I don't like seeing my wife hurt, so if that means acting like a *super-cowboy,* I'll do what needs to be done."

"Richard. I'm not—We're—"

He shushes me, "Can you not do that? Can't you just let me be your knight in shining armor right now?"

I let out a breath, "Knights in shining armor don't exist, Richard."

"That's because their armor is dirty from all the times they protect their princess." Richard says back. I try to hold back the tears that immediately well in my eyes, I look at him as his chest rises and falls, his arms still strongly holding me.

"Richard." I say in a whisper as our lips meet in a tender moment. I'm unsure of who kissed who. Maybe it had been me; maybe his arms curled me up to him until our lips met, but the moment our lips parted, the horses we rode on sprint away. I wonder if Shadow pulled

Mocha-Donna into the sprint as their reins keep them together, the same way they pulled us out of the moment.

I step out of my husband's arms as he helps me up at the same time. Both of us look out at the horses getting smaller in the distance they run. The walk to the barn isn't far, but I'm scared to admit that I'm forced to spend the entire walk with Richard. I gulp as I just barely look at him to see my husband already looking at me.

"Ready to walk it, or do you need a minute?" His deep voice is almost in tune with the thunder that comes right after his question. We both look up at the sky as dark clouds hang above us.

"We should definitely make a run for it." I answer as our eyes meet. I try not to look at the rest of him, not with him wearing that ridiculous cowboy hat that somehow makes him look ten times sexier than I already find my husband. Richard smirks.

"Race you there?"

I'm about to answer his rhetorical question with my obvious response when he begins to run.

"Hey!" I yell as I run after him, watching as he holds the hat to his head as he runs, the storm just starting with sprinkles of water hitting us as we finally make it to the barn. The air already has the aroma of a rainstorm as I look at the stalls holding three of the six horses on the property. The sound of the rain hits the tin roof when I finally notice Richard standing still, his chest puffing out slightly, as his eyes follow my every movement. I'm a bit mad that he couldn't be bothered to look at me when it mattered most.

"What's your plan with us?" He asks, breaking the silence between us; the rain's tip taps get louder, drowning out any silence between us. I can't run away; I can only just try to change the subject.

"I thought we weren't talking about that." I say as a Mocha-Donna gallops in between us before she quickly finds an empty stall to shake the rain out of her hair. I look at Richard to see him scratch his jawline; he sighs as I watch his jaw flex.

"I'm trying to save our marriage here. I just need to know how far you're taking this. Am I that bad? Have you truly been that unhappy with me? Are you out of love with me?"

His questions made me watery-eyed, "I don't want to break your heart." My voice almost croaks as I let my knuckles wipe tears that don't fall from my eyes.

Richard breaks apart any space between us, getting so close to me that my neck strains slightly to look at him.

"You breaking my heart is the least of my concerns. Do you still love me?"

My tears break through, "Yes. Stupidly, ridiculously and monumentally." I finish right as our lips collide into each other. I hum as Richard picks me up and my legs wrap around him; his arms carry me until my back meets a wall. Richard's tongue darts between my lips, making me feel limp in his arms. My lips weaken as our tongues meet and play in each other's mouths.

We only part when Richard lips kiss down my chin, following my jawline and down my neck. I moan in the haze of my eyesight; the sound of the heavy rain drowns out the world around us. Richard's lips and the feel of his hands on my ass holding me has my pussy wet with need, and I'm a desperate woman. I'm desperate for my husband to be inside me with the way his tongue circles on my neck as he sucks the skin into his mouth.

I moan his name as my hands travel down his arms and hold on tight as I grind my pelvis into him. He grumbles into my skin, pushing himself into me, as I feel the growth of him in his pants. I want him to take me without me having to ask for it. I want it to last; I want him to explode inside me as soon as possible. Richard's lips and tongue make it back to mine, and I kiss him desperately, forcing my tongue to tangle with his.

Richard's lips part from mine just as a moan escapes my throat, begging him for more.

"I want you, Amelia. I know things are..." He pauses as he looks at me with a stern expression, his throat bobbing, "You've wanted me—you've had me all across this country, but now it's time for me to have you in this barn."

It's exactly what I wanted, as our lips fall back into each other, our tongues entwining together as I feel him put me down slowly. Both of us grabbed at each other's jeans to unbutton them and pull them down. Richard pulls on my belt loop before I'm able to get them off.

I wanted to question him, but I let him lead me to where a saddle sat on a sawhorse. I face him as he pulls down my pants; finally, he follows suit, taking his jeans and throwing them off to the side. Richard's cock juts out just slightly from his briefs; I can't help but stare until he pulls my hair lightly to look up at him. I lean lightly on the saddle as he begins to speak.

"I don't know how I could go this long without seeing you like this, Turtle. You're so fucking beautiful." His words cut off as his mouth crashed down on mine just long enough that I pulled at his henley, getting him closer as our tongues swirled around, before he removed the rest of his clothing. He tugged at my shirt enough times until I caved, shedding it and my bra, sucking in a breath as our bodies came back together in a slapping sound.

I could feel the insecurity of my naked body in front of his breathtaking, godlike sculpted body. Every part of Richard I touched felt like he had at least five muscles in that area; I could only imagine how he saw me. With both of our bodies naked, he turns me around and leans me over the saddle, his cock just barely pressing into my center. I hold onto the sides of the saddle as he pushes himself deeper inside me.

Both of us groan as he fucks me from behind. I feel like I'm holding onto the saddle with all of my strength as he pounds into me. I feel my sweat drip down me as the rain continues to grow louder around us. I feel my pussy tighten around him as he fucks me harder; I only stiffen when his hands grip onto the part of my body I'm self-conscious about. The area just above my waist I used to love, now I feel the flab, the rolls that his fingers sink into. I try not to think of it as he picks up the pace. I have to stop myself from thinking of it as I feel Richard hold me harder; his groan reminds me that he's about to come.

Richard doesn't pull out or stop himself; instead, I feel his cock pump back in and out until it pulses, until he's filled me with his cum. Part of me is still surprised that he comes inside me, but the other part of me, a smaller part, tells me it means something. I wonder if that something is a change in him or if I'm reading too much into it.

Chapter Fifteen

Richard – Present

Coming inside Amelia feels therapeutic, like I've been set free from the prison inside my mind. I've been putting so much pressure on myself, working hard for what we've built and hiding behind baseball. I know she doesn't fully get it yet, but I want her too. I want her to get why I've been distant, but I don't see it working out in my favor. It's too hard to talk about it even now; I can just hope one day it will be easy.

Keeping Amelia has always been my priority; watching her slip away has nearly killed me. The longer I view her as someone other than mine, the more depressed I become. I can't have her falling in love with someone else; I can't live in a world where it's not us, where it's not Richard and Amelia against the world. Everything that's happened has felt like the beginning of the worst nightmare of my life.

My wife dresses before me, and I'm trying hard not to touch her. I'm trying hard not to show her how badly I need her, but it's so hard. Everything about Amelia is so addicting; no matter what she thinks happened between us, I'd never let anything like that happen. I want to call myself an addict for my wife, but it's further than that; I'm obsessed—the kind of husband that would stalk his wife if it meant I was protecting her too.

The two of us walk back to the house the moment the rain subsides; never had we been so quiet, not even when I fucked her in the barn, were we this quiet. The sounds of our slapping skin, her heavy breaths as she moaned my name, my growl as I came inside of her. Now things had been awkward, the silence heavier than the tension we both carried. Whatever she held to her chest was bigger than a simple fuck; it was bigger than the both of us, which meant it was her everything.

After I opened the back door for Amelia, both of us walked into her house. Part of me hoped no one was home, for the fact that she didn't actively turn me away for once. I imagined we'd have a chance to talk, though a part of me knew that talking might lead to me having her again. My cock tensed at the thought while my mouth salivated, I hadn't tasted my wife in so long, and I couldn't wait to have her dripping wet all over my face.

"Ramsey." My thoughts of taking my wife in every space of the house vanished upon hearing Graves' voice welcome me into their home.

"Graves." I say with a tight-lipped smile. He doesn't bother to even try to remain civil in front of his sister; I can just see the anger fuming off his body; his eyes are murderous every time he looks in my direction.

"Amelia." A voice calls from behind Graves; I wouldn't have noticed the redhead if she didn't walk around Graves to greet my wife.

"Chelsea." My wife's voice sounds surprised to see her friend. I remember the first time the two of them met when Chelsea dated Christian, I remember the two of them hitting it off before everything changed, they had hung out a few times outside of the stadium games. The redhead blushes when she and Graves make eye contact.

"Hi Ramsey." Chelsea says, averting her eyes from him as she makes her way to hug my wife.

"What are you doing here?" Amelia asks as the two separate from their hug.

"Girls night? Did you forget?"

Amelia looks back at me as if I'm the reason for her forgetting. I stand there waiting for her to answer her friend.

"Um. No." She responds, looking back at Chelsea. We watch as Chelsea pulls something from Amelia's hair—a brown leaf.

"What's this?" Chelsea asks with a chuckle as she looks between me and Ames. Amelia is quick to snatch the little leaf out of her hand.

"Nothing. Help me get ready?" Amelia grabs her friend's hand and leads her out of the room, leaving Graves and me to stand in silence. It's not uncomfortable, not as both of us pull out our phones and pretend we're not in each other's company.

Twenty minutes go by before Amelia and Chelsea exit her room, Amelia in the shortest dress I've ever seen. Chelsea seemed to have curled my wife's hair as well; perhaps it was her idea for Amelia to wear the sparkly red dress with dark red lipstick. Either way, my cock wants to react to my wife's breasts nearly busting out of the top of the dress, and I bet if she turned around it would be the same for her ass. I want to throw my wife over my shoulder and take her to her room, eat her pussy and watch her suck my dick with that lipstick staining my skin.

"Richard." Amelia says to snap me out of staring at her body. The smirk on her face says it all, "I'm sorry we didn't get to... talk more. But I'm going out with Chelsea, so maybe we can talk another day?"

I nod in answer, "Of course."

"Have fun, you two." Graves says, winking at both his sister and her friend.

"Not too much fun." I let my words follow quickly after.

Chelsea nods as she helps Amelia out the front door as she follows her, shutting the door slowly.

"You fucked her in the barn, didn't you?" I look over at Graves, whose eyes have barely looked up from his phone, but he looks at me just as I answer.

"And what if I did?"

"She's trying to detox from you, not get back on your bullshit."

"There is no bullshit, you don't even know what you're talking about."

"Oh, I do; I know everything. You think my sister doesn't talk? I've heard everything she's said to her new friends, AKA my best friends. Tanner and Luke have told me all about you and all the shit you put her through. Whatever you think this is, it's ten times worse. You need to leave her alone."

"You know, it can go both ways, right?"

"No, it can't, Rich. She fucking loves you, you idiot. She hates you at the same time. She can't fucking deal with this; you are bad for her. You've ruined her."

I gulp, "That's not true."

"You want a fucking bet? I can call up either one of them, and they'll tell me all over again. The only reason I know any of it is because they're afraid of me." He says, ready to continue, "You need to get the fuck out of here before you break her more than she already is."

The silence that passes between us is astronomic, the rage is even worse. My brows furrow as I look at Amelia's brother, as protective as he is of her, I'm worse.

"I'm not leaving. I'm not going anywhere, Graves. You want to make it fight? Put up your fists, and I'll prove to you that I belong here."

Graves huffs, "Outside. Now."

I know he means business the moment he doesn't even give me a second to respond to him, he just starts walking to the door. Worse is that it's the front door, meaning he means business, he wouldn't fight me in front of the animals to avoid them getting spooked, so the moment the front door closes, I know I'm in for a real beating.

Chapter Sixteen

Amelia – Present

"Did you see the way he looked at you?" Chelsea asked with a laugh as we drank our cosmos. They weren't my favorite drink, but she swore they'd get us drunk faster, and that was the biggest selling point.

"It's a bit hard not to notice when my husband looks at me." I answer with a sip of my drink.

"Your *husband*? Girl, why are you still calling him that? I thought you were trying to move on?" I watch her hair shake with her head, "Do you need me to kick him in the balls for you?"

I scoff, realizing my friend is already close to the drunk stage, "Can I ask you something without you getting offended?"

"I'm not the type to get offended, you know this. Hit me. But not literally." Chelsea said with a chuckle.

"Okay, you're drunk." I move her glass away from her as she reaches for it.

"No no no. I'm buzzed, there's a difference. I feel good, and I need you to talk to me. So ask me anything."

"You're here to take care of me, right? Like obviously you're trying to make sure Richard goes back to Florida, but you're here right now, for what? Are you just sticking around to make sure I'm okay?"

Chelsea's eyes go wide as she brings her glass back to her lips and downs the rest of her cosmo.

"Chels."

"I plead the first."

"It's actually the fifth, hon."

"Shit." She looks around and raises her hand, getting a waiter's attention. I want to scold her for not having proper manners, but the second I turn to see the waiter, he's smiling and walking over, two drinks already in his hands for us.

"Oh my god, Chels!"

"What? I told him to refresh our drinks if he sees they're low."

"Yeah, did you give him a hefty tip for that?" I ask with wide eyes.

Chelsea shrugs, "I told him I'd give him a good time at the end of the night."

"You're not serious?" I want to say she's not serious, but as the waiter sets our drinks down, she winks at him and purposefully exposes her cleavage a little more when he bends to scoot her drink towards her. The waiter leaves, and I give her my only mom-face I know to make.

Chelsea clicks her lips, "Please, once you're single for a while, you'll understand the struggle."

The moment she says the words, is the moment I feel a sour taste in my mouth. Single. I don't want to be single. Not really. I want to be with my husband and him to make me happy, but the fact that I'm not happy with him has me wanting to change everything. Ever since I

119

started my journey with the guys to get me back to being healthy both mentally and physically, I've been really trying not to think about my future, the idea of being divorced doesn't settle my stomach, nor does the idea of calling myself single.

"Ames?"

"Yeah?"

"Do you want to tell me everything? You don't have to, but I'm curious to know if there's more that you were leaving out. It feels like there is." She was right, I had just given her the cliffnotes of what happened.

I gave her the details, letting the drinks refill through my story. Both of us were nearly in tears by the time I finished telling her everything. I try not to look at her as I wipe the corners of my eyes, making sure not to smudge my eyeliner. Chelsea might've done the same, the moment we look at each other, we smile lightly.

"Maybe we should head home, we almost cried... In a bar. Nobody needs to see us like this." She says, grabbing her glass and downing the last of her drink. "Let's get out of here."

I chuckle because she's right, we pay our tab quickly and get out of there before the waiter she owed her body to found us. The cab I ordered to pick us up comes, and I expect us to have some quiet down time in the car ride back to my house.

"I feel guilty." Chelsea says the moment the cab starts driving. She faces me, so I turn to face her.

"Why? Thinking you led the waiter on?"

Chelsea shakes her head, "I feel like I'm partially responsible for everything that happened with Ramsey."

"How? That's silly."

"Maybe it is, but you told me your story in confidence, and now all I can think about is that I don't think any of Ramsey's teammates would ever talk badly about you. Everyone knew you were pregnant, so they knew that you were due, and when you didn't have the baby, it just made them talk about that. I know because a few of them came to me for the facts. It's not like they could ask you or Ramsey. He would've killed them, and you stopped coming to the games."

"Chels–"

"Some of them were actually hoping you'd come back to the games, they wanted you to know we had your back and that we'd be your village if you needed anything. And I'm sorry, but they only knew that because of me and my big, fat mouth telling them your family lived in California. So I fucked up there. I'm sure you really did hear some bad things because there were a few mean people calling you fat, but they were jealous and really big idiots for saying it so close to you. But we're a community that has each other's back, and I was ready to do that for you—until..."

I try hard not to cry, "Until you broke up with Christian?"

Chelsea cries, "Yeah. It really changed my perspective when I saw it from your side. I couldn't exactly go back with everyone knowing how we ended, and with the job here in California, it just didn't make sense to defend myself to the team. I'm sure I was talked about too."

I sob, pulling my friend into me, giving her an embrace that both of us have needed.

"I don't blame you, I'm sorry if I made you feel guilty." I say with a hitch in my throat.

"I'm sorry if I am to blame, but I'm also sorry for not telling you sooner." Our hug tightens as we feel the cab come to a stop.

"Is this your house?" The driver asks. We both separated to look out the window, but instead of just seeing the farmhouse in our view, we saw my brother fighting with my husband.

"Oh my god!" Chelsea said as Graves threw a punch right into Richard's face.

I don't remember anything in the rush of getting out of the car to make it in between my family fighting, but the second I get close, Chelsea stops me with a hand on my shoulder.

"What are you doing?" She whispers as they throw more punches at each other. Richard going down before Graves does. I rip her hand off me and run to my husband.

"Richard." I make it to him just to see blood running down his nose, bruises already showing up, "Oh my god, are you okay?"

He groans as he begins to get up, "I'm fine. I can keep going."

"N-no. Sit down." My voice shakes as he gets to his full height, "Richard, please."

His blue eyes look down at me, "I have to do this, Turtle."

"You guys are going to kill each other."

"Just add it to my bill."

"Richard, that doesn't make sense." I say pressing my hands on his chest, I can feel his heart beating way too fast. "Please, don't do this."

"What am I supposed to do? Your brother has made it clear he doesn't care if I live or die, he says it's better if I'm dead so I can't break your heart. So I'll let him, but I won't go down without a fight."

My brother growls as he charges at Richard, Richard pushes me out of the way, not hard enough for me to fall. I scream at my brother to stop. Chelsea approaches me as I run back to the two of them on the ground, Richard holding Graves' arms from punching him.

"Graves! Please stop!" I cry, "Richard!"

"Dammit, Amelia, get out of here!" My brother yells at me.

Richard groans, he looks like he's been beaten to all hell, almost half-dead just by the blood and bruises all over his face, and I haven't even seen the rest of his body to determine how injured he truly is.

"Didn't you hear my wife? She said stop!" Richard groans as he overpowers my brother and gets them to roll, this time Richard towering over Graves.

"Richard..." I sob his name as I watch him hold my brother's hands and arms from hurting him.

"Get off of me." Graves spits on Richard's face, I watch as Richard lets go of my brother and punches the grass next to his face. I jump and feel goosebumps as Richard screams.

It takes me a minute to realize that Richard stands and walks over my brother to get to me. I look at the hurt in his eyes as his dirty fingers wipe away my tears.

"I only want you to be happy. I'll repeat every day spent without you if it means you're the happiest you've ever been." His words sounded even more sincere with the look on his face, even with the bloodied split lip. I want to kiss him for saying those words. I want to be happy, I want him to make me happy, and that's the hardest part of it all. I look down at his left hand, the one that punched the ground, and pull it up to my lips. Richard winces as I kiss his wounds, just feeling his hand, I can tell it has to be broken.

"Can I fix this?" I still feel the adrenaline of watching the two people I care about most fight.

"You're the only one that can fix me, Amelia." Richard hums. I sigh, wanting to cry all over again; instead, I look at my brother, who's spitting out blood, while my friend looks confused and worried all at the same time.

"I'm gonna drive Ramsey to my parents house and take care of him there." I say to both Graves and Chelsea, neither of them answer me as I walk to my brother's truck.

The time before I came home seemed like a blur, from being buzzed to sober within minutes. Both of us get in the car and drive in the slow hum of the truck.

"Don't go to sleep." I say to Richard as I look at the time, almost midnight, "You could be concussed."

He hums, "That means he'd have to hit me hard enough."

I roll my eyes and sigh as I continue driving the dirt road.

"I'm sorry if I ruined your girls' night."

I look at him through my periphery, "You didn't ruin it."

"Well, it couldn't have been much fun if I didn't ruin it for you."

"It was a collaborative effort between you and my brother." I say back, focusing on the road.

Richard chuckles, "Right."

"So were you just going to fight him to the death?"

"Would you really care if he did beat me to death?"

That gets me to slam on the breaks, "Are you kidding?"

He looks shocked for just a moment before he winces in pain.

"You're still my husband, Richard."

"He's your brother—"

"I love you, you idiot. Nothing my brother has ever said has ever changed my mind about you. I love my brother, but his attitude towards you is not even your fault. His protection over me is too much, we're grown adults. Neither of you should be fighting like this. We're almost forty."

"I'd do it again." Richard mumbles.

"What?"

"I'd do it all over again if it means hearing you say that you still love me."

"Richard, you'd break your hand, get pulverized for that? Do you hear yourself?"

"I don't want to break your heart, so if it means I get hurt to make sure I don't do it, I'll take whatever your brother can throw at me."

I start to drive again, trying to let it all sink in. Everything from tonight has thrown me for a loop, and I don't know how to handle any of it. I can only hope he understands why I've done everything I've done... The moment I reach my parents house, we get in the house quietly, and I take him to the bathroom. My parents first aid kit was always in the same place, even at the farmhouse; they always kept it under the sink, complete with a splint. I clean up his wounds and splint his hand, hoping it'll help until he sees a doctor.

Richard's dominant hand grabs mine as I finish up the cut on his eyebrow, his blue eyes damning me to swim in them. I gulp as I let go of his hand, trying to remind myself how tonight could've gone if I hadn't come home early. I can only imagine what he thinks of me.

"Did you—Um. Did you meet any guys tonight?" He asks, looking like he's got something to be afraid of.

"N-no." I rolled my eyes at the thought of my conversation with Chelsea, "I kind of cried in the bar. No guys are really attracted to that."

"Oh. Is everything okay?"

I answered quickly, "Yeah. I mean, I don't know. I just know I'm not ready for that. Moving on..."

I rest my hand on his cheek, making sure the spot there is a bruise and not just dirt, I rub my thumb over the spot, Richard doesn't wince at my movement, instead, I feel his hand reach up to rub my chin. My lips part the more his thumb pulls my chin down. I'm barely able to get his name out as our lips meet, I hardly think of the cut on his lip as our tongues meet, and my hands immediately feel him up. He groans as he pulls me closer, our bodies close enough for me to press myself up against him and feel his length underneath his pants.

"Richard? You out there?" My dad calls from the other room.

Our lips pull apart, both of us out of breath as my husband clears his throat,

"Yeah. Just washing up before I head to bed."

"Alright. Sleep well." My dad says before we hear a door close. The heat of the moment has passed as I look at my husband's lip, bleeding slightly. I take a towel and press it to the wound.

"I should let you get some sleep."

"What about my concussion?"

I sigh with a slight smile passing across my face, "I think you're fine."

"I'd rather have your company."

"My parents will kill me if they find us in the room across from them."

"You can leave in the morning?" Even as Richard offers it, I feel the pain of that idea. Every time I walk away from him, it gets harder...

"It's not a good idea, Richard." I pause, hoping he can read my expression, "I'm going to go, you rest and get better, okay?"

I watch as he rolls his eyes and lets his head fall back against the bathroom wall, "Okay."

"Bye." I say as I start to walk out, he grabs my hand and pulls me back, our lips almost touching.

"Not bye, not ever that. I'll see you tomorrow, my love."

I feel my chest tighten, "See you tomorrow, then." I blink as his grip loosens on me. I leave before I do something stupid, like stay and make love to my husband in my parents house...

Chapter Seventeen

Richard – Present

Coming up to the farm wasn't an easy task, especially when there was a reasonable hike from her parents house to the farmhouse. It wasn't bad, but I hadn't had a great cardio workout within the time I had been in California. I wasn't used to the heat here, I wasn't used to the hills or walking up a path that was intended for one truck at a time, not a two-lane road. Even walking on gravel had been a bit difficult for me. My workouts had always been in a gym. Cardio especially, with the way Florida heat was, the humidity there was worse than anywhere I'd traveled to so far. Cardio on a treadmill was way different than walking the almost thirty minutes to the farmhouse. By the time I made it up the steps and to the door, I was ready to ask for eighty ounces of water.

"You're not pizza." Graves said, answering the door.

"And you're not my wife."

My brother-in-law smirked, "She's not here."

"Where is she, then?"

I hear his tongue click against the roof of his mouth, "Trust me, bro. You do not want to know." He looks at me with a haughty expression, like he knows and he wants to tell me, but he wants to rub it in my face first.

I hold back a growl despite feeling my chest vibrate, "I can handle it."

"She's on a date."

My brows furrow, "Right. You expect me to believe that?"

"I don't have a reason to lie to you, especially when you totally need to be brought down a peg or two."

"I thought we were past this—"

"Never gonna happen. As long as my sister's pissed, I'm pissed. When she's unhappy, I am."

With a scoff, I spoke, "You're not twins. This isn't a game of you taking her side or mine."

"You're right, *Richard*, it's not. It's me defending my sister. I'm always going to take my sister's side, we're blood. You're just a friend who fucked me over."

My growl escapes me as Graves slams the door on my face. I pound at the door, pissed as hell. If I had known I was coming here for Amelia's brother, I'd have worn something less nice and something more...rippable.

"What?!" Graves shouts as he forcefully opens the door again.

"I didn't fuck you over, you dick! If you knew me at all, you'd know it wasn't me who didn't stick up for you. You'd know it was Ripley. I was there, I know. I'm the one who told coach to put you out on that field, I'm the one who did everything to try and get you out there for those scouts. But fucking Ripley and his big ass mouth came in and said you weren't ready. He said you had your bags packed if we didn't win. You and I both know that Kyle cheated his way into the league. If he didn't fuck you over, he'd be doing it to someone else."

"You expect me to believe that shit?" Graves' brows dip, "Ripley's my teammate, do you understand what could happen if that were true?"

"I didn't know he was on your team until last year. I didn't even know you two were friends."

Graves spits, "We're not. I'm not friends with anyone... Except for the two idiots that live with me."

"I'm telling you the truth, man. Believe it or not, Kyle's never been a good dude. I thought you knew that? He's always been after everything I've had, especially in the game. I bet that's why he did what he did with you and the scouts, because he wouldn't be able to handle that both, me and my best bud, got in the majors together at the same time."

Graves face sours at my words. He looks away from me, but I can tell he's thinking about it, connecting the dots, and he either realizes his mistake or how right I've been. When he looks back at me, his eyes widen.

"What?" I ask with twisted brows.

"Shit, we need to go right now." Graves grabs the keys off the entry table and slams the door as he walks past me to his truck. I take no time catching up with him.

"What, why? Where are we going?"

"My sister—your wife is on a date with Ripley right fucking now."

My eyes grow wide as I feel anger burning, the sliver of doubt from earlier has disappeared, now I'm enraged, now I feel my blood boiling with a furious flame that won't be blown out without a fight.

"I'm driving." My brother-in-law says as we reach the car.

"Good, I'd probably drive right into that motherfucker's house if I drove right now." Graves looks over at me, his anger seems to halt as he gives me a look, one I'm not sure he's ever given me before. It's a weird sight, a weird feeling when his hand lands on my shoulder.

"We're gonna get your wife back."

By the time we made it to the worst place in the world, the drive-in, we immediately started searching for Kyle's car. I'm unsure where to start as Graves just begins, opening doors of strangers' cars and shutting them quickly. It should be a sign that this guy would go to bat for me even when he still hates me. As positive as that is, I'm not all that sure that we'll be able to find Amelia in time. I start looking right before I notice a little red convertible with the back of the head of a woman who reminds me too much of Amelia. I watch as the guy in the driver's seat wraps an arm around her, like it's normal for him to do, but the moment the woman's hand reaches to remove his arm, I take my shot. I run towards the convertible.

"Amelia!" I say, she quickly looks at me.

"Richard?"

"Ames!" Her brother calls from the other side, as he walks over to us.

"Graves?"

"What the hell is going on here?" Kyle asks with brows quirked. "You guys realize we're on a date, right?"

"No, you're not." I say with a growl.

"No, we're not." Amelia says at the same time to him. "I told you, we're here as friends."

"Right, because you say yes to a romcom at the drive-in and are just okay with sharing one popcorn with me."

"I was being considerate and being a little frugal. Is that such a bad thing?" She asks no one in particular.

"Get out of the car, Amelia, we're going." I grab the handle for the car.

"Get your sticky hands off my car." Kyle says with gritted teeth, as his hand dares to land on my wife's leg.

"Get your fucking hands off my wife, you douchebag."

Amelia's hands go up in defeat before she gets out of the car herself, "What the fuck is wrong with you two?"

"He's mad that I'm dating you." Kyle says as I talk over him.

"He's trying to steal you away from me."

Amelia chuckles, "What? For one, Kyle, I told you we're not dating. This was a one-time thing."

"Second if you count the club." He winks at her. I want to run at him, but he sits in his car, looking smug. Amelia puts a hand on my chest to stop me from grabbing the guy and choking him to death.

"And two." She pushes on my chest, but the glare I have for Ripley is full-forced, "Two." Amelia says, pulling my face to look at her, "No one, *no one* could steal me away from my husband."

My chest heaves, my heart constricts, my pulse slowing down from her touch, from the way her eyes stare back at me. The fire douses with her soft lips as she presses them to mine. The kiss is brief, and not as long as I'd like, but Amelia's the one to remind me we're in public, in a place filled with cars and people in them.

"So that's it? This is over, like that?" Kyle asks as if Amelia gave him hope.

"Kyle—"

"Uh-huh. You've said enough, Ames. It's time for me to say something." Graves says stepping in.

Kyle looks at him with a smile, "What's up, bud?"

Graves doesn't need to take a breath for what he says to him, "Did you really think I wouldn't find out that you were the reason why it took me an extra two years to get into the majors? Did you actually think you and I would be okay once I found out from my brother-in-law? And lastly, have you ever considered what it would be like to have me on your bad side?"

Kyle audibly gulps or gasps, it's something I never heard from a man's voice before.

"Get the fuck out of here before I show you exactly how I got my name." Graves growls right before Kyle's car starts. I step back, pulling Amelia with me.

We watch as Ripley backs out of the space and drives off. I want to smile and say that Graves truly got him good. Watching Kyle scamper with his tail between his legs is a victory I never saw coming.

"You got your name from Grampa Graves. What story were you exactly going to tell him if he stayed?" Amelia asks, looking over at her brother.

"The same one Gramps told me. That he killed enough people in his past life as a marine to know exactly two hundred different ways to kill a man and where to hide the body."

I watch as Amelia pinches the bridge of her nose, "He—Graves, Grandpa wasn't even in the Marines."

"That's not true. He told me stories, he showed me plenty of his badges." Her brother shoots back with a questionable expression.

She rolls her eyes, "Oh my god, Graves, those were a part of his Halloween costume."

"N-no. No, that can't be."

Amelia can't help but grin, a silent chuckle escaping her that only I can hear. I look at her, her eyes glistening as our gazes meet, and I brush my lips against her forehead.

"We should probably get out of here." I say to my wife; she nods in response.

We walk hand in hand as her brother walks behind us, still putting together the past he had with his grandpa.

"You thought I was on a date." Amelia says with the push of her hips into me.

"Hell yeah, I did. If you saw the way his hands were on you, you'd think so too."

I look at the small smile on her lips, "I like it when you're protective."

I let out a low hum, "That was more than protective, Amelia, I was ready to commit a crime." A murder in particular, but I don't need to say that to see the look in my wife's eyes.

"Almost animalistic." She doesn't have to smirk to read in between the lines. I turn to her and get myself as close to her as possible. Our faces are close enough I'd kiss her again, but it would be raw and powerful. Graves isn't far behind us, so teasing her will just have to do.

"Is that what you like, Amelia? Do you like seeing me act like an animal, overprotective, jealous to the point of doing anything to make sure you're in my arms?" I don't have to have my arms around her or my hands on her to know that my wife is wet and needy for me. Amelia's breath is uneven as I take my time teasing her. As we wait at the truck, I watch her gaze flick up and down, as if she can't choose whether to stare into my eyes or kiss me. Neither of us are able to make a move when Graves yells.

"Hey! What is this that I'm seeing? You tell me grandpa wasn't a veteran, and now you're eye-fucking my best friend in the parking lot of a drive-in."

Amelia rolls her eyes and looks at her brother, "Of course not. Can we go home now?"

I opened the door for her to let her in first, "Tonight was interesting." Amelia says as she takes my hand to help herself into the truck.

"It was?"

"You almost punched a guy, and my brother called you his best friend. Things are looking up for you, Ramsey." She winks. I scooch in next to her.

"I hope so, Turtle." I say softly as her brother climbs in on the driver's side.

"I bet I missed my pizza delivery..." Graves sighs as he starts the truck.

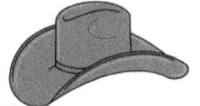

Chapter Eighteen

Richard – Past

AMELIA (19), RICHARD (21)

"How could they do this to us? Do they realize that we have the potential to be on the same team?" Graves growls as he reads the newsletter from our university.

"Can you blame that they think you both are that good? Shouldn't you guys be happy that you're tied in that section?" Amelia says with a small smile as she puts plates of food down in front of us.

"I'm not sure I can eat, Turtle." I say, pushing the plate into the center of the table. "We both worked hard, yes. But to have us butt-heads is a whole other thing. They know we're practically siblings, and now we're being put in a position that can fuck up our careers if we do something wrong."

"Is being tied for MOP that big of a deal?" My ignorant but sweet wife asks.

"Yes." Both me and her brother answer at the same time.

Amelia rolls her eyes at us as Graves throws down the paper.

"So now our next game we'll have scouts out there looking at both of us, not just there for our title, but to see who is better." Graves scowls, "This is bullshit."

"That I get. But Most Outstanding Player is such a high achievement, I'm pretty sure they will take both of you." Amelia says with not a lick of understanding of the game we play.

Her brother avoids her words by digging into his breakfast, not looking up at either of us as his eyes stay glued to the paper.

"Hey, remember when I promised that I would learn about farm life for you?" I ask her with a loving smile.

"Yes." She looks at me with a small smirk on her face, "And you've done a pretty good job so far. I mean, you're not mixing up the veggies and seeds anymore."

My brows drop, "Listen, how was I supposed to know the difference between the bags? They're so similar."

"One has a picture of a rooster on it, and the other one has a cornucopia of vegetables." Graves says monotonous, still not looking up at us.

"The point you're trying to make?" Amelia's brows lift up as she takes a bite from her own plate.

"I think maybe it's time you learn some things about professional baseball, college version included. What do you think about that?"

"So you get to learn about what I love to do, and I get to learn what you love to do?" She hums, "Seems fair, but only if we get to compare notes after."

"Notes? What kind of notes?"

Amelia scoots in closer to me, letting a hand travel down my chest to my—I cough to clear my throat. My cock twitches after her hand had lightly grazed it through my clothes.

"Those notes! Yes, yes. We definitely can compare notes. We could start right now if you want." Amelia chuckles at my answer.

"Just don't have sex in my room, please." Her brother spits out, despite his inability to look up at us, he sure understands context clues.

Amelia and I look at each other, the glint in her eyes says she's ready to take me up on my offer. As much as I want to stay and finish my breakfast, I only want one thing, and that is the space in between my wife's thighs.

"Where's Graves?" My college coach asks me as he pulls me back into the dugout. It'd been a rough game. We'd been tied with this team before, but this one meant more, especially with the scouts in the bleachers.

"He's not here?" My brows crease, "That's not possible, he wouldn't miss—"

"I'm not asking for his life story, Greene. Anyone know where he is?" The coach spits. My other teammate and the one guy no one truly likes walks over to us.

"I heard he was taking one for the team." Ripley says with a blank expression.

"What?" Both me and the coach ask simultaneously.

"Yeah. He said he wasn't ready. Said that we should go on without him." Kyle continues.

"No, no fucking way. Coach, Graves would never say that. He's here, he'll be here. Just let me find him—"

Kyle talks over me, "He told me his bags are packed and that if we lose this game, he's walking away."

I look over at Ripley, hoping he understands that I will kill him if he doesn't stop talking.

"Do you really think he'd miss being here when there's scouts for him?" I ask our coach, hoping he ignores everything Kyle has said.

Coach groans, "Where the fuck is he then? Patience is wearing thin, and we're almost in our ninth inning."

"I'm telling you, he's not coming. You can put me in, coach." Kyle says with a wicked grin.

"Please. Give Graves an extra minute."

The time we had until the ninth inning passed, all of my calls to Graves had gone straight to the answering machine. Even when Kyle looked pleased, I kept trying to get ahold of my friend, my brother-in-law, my teammate. He was supposed to be the one to challenge me, and he wasn't there. It wasn't supposed to be me versus Ripley, he was more of my rival than the team we were up against.

Coach's voice ripped me out of my thoughts, "Ripley, you're up."

Graves would kill me if he'd ever find out..

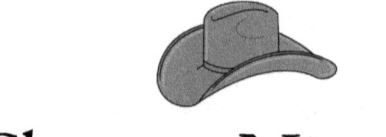

Chapter Nineteen

Amelia – Present

The doorbell rings in the middle of my bite of my donut. Whoever had brought them deserved a big hug; with no one around, I just hoped they were for anyone in the house. The ring of the doorbell goes off one more time as I look at myself. My poor excuse for jean shorts keeps riding up my thighs the moment I take two steps towards the door. The oversized shirt I wore was a relic of Richard's university days; it was considered mine over a decade ago. Perhaps it was time to remind myself of my relationship status with my husband, but as the doorbell rang, the thought flew further from my mind. Leading him on was not my intention, but the history between us and the way we knew each other was too strong not to resist.

"Ames!" Chelsea shouts the moment I open the door; I'm only slightly surprised by her presence. I shouldn't be surprised with how much she's invited herself over since she'd been visiting.

"Chels!" I said once I swallowed my bite, "What's up?"

"We're day drinking!" She answers, pulling a bottle of alcohol out of her large tote bag.

"Oh, so *you're* day drinking?"

She shushed me, "*We* are too. Now that I'm here, we can get started!" Chelsea smiles before fully barging into my house. She makes a beeline for the kitchen as I follow her and stuff the rest of my donut in my mouth.

Tanner walks out of his room just in time to see me and Chelsea making mixed drinks—more than three shots of vodka with a small splash of soda. Both of us with donuts in one hand while we pour with the other, look at Tanner as he looks surprised at first but then smirks.

"Count me in, girls. After this week, I need something to fix my love life."

"Trouble in paradise?" Chelsea asks with a mouth full of a donut. Tanner and I look at each other.

"Something like that." He coughs, "You gonna add enough soda to that?" The glug of the vodka bottle sloshes as Chelsea turns it right side up. There's barely enough of a shot left as she puts the bottle to her lips and gulps the rest of it down.

By the time she removes the bottle from her lips, she speaks, "I haven't had sex in over five months. I am fiending for a man. A great burly hell of a man; the meaner the better, the hotter the better. I can't even tell you how badly I need it. My vibrator can't even satisfy me anymore."

I chuckle at her sentence as my friend looks me up and down.

"It's funny to you because despite your separation, you're still banging your husband." She rolls her eyes and picks up her cup and starts drinking. Tanner gives me a look like he's disappointed in me as I pick up my own drink to cover the fact that I have no shame for fucking my husband. I shouldn't have, but it's so hard to stop when my husband looks the way he does, when he knows all the spots that turn me on, especially when we're fucking like we used to before everything happened.

"Sitting inside and drinking is depressing; let's go sit on the porch and drink like real old people would." Tanner says before either of us down whatever is left in our cups.

The second we make it onto the back porch, all of us manage to fit on the swing with our drinks before we drink like there's no tomorrow. We briefly talked about how our weeks were going, and Chelsea managed to convince me to get a massage with her, but after chatting we fell into a comfortable silence, just drinking and laughing about nothing. Not until Luke came out and saw us drinking.

"You guys seem like an unlikely trio. Why do I feel like you guys could be up to no good?" Lucas asked, looking between me and Tanner, a blush growing on him the second I notice them looking at each other.

"We're just day drinking, nothing horrible." Tanner answers before taking a sip of his drink. Chelsea must notice it too because her eyes go wide when Lucas looks down at Tanner before focusing back on me.

Luke's jaw clenches. "Your *husband* asked for my help on the farm today."

"*He did?*" I ask without bothering to correct him. "What for?"

"Apparently he needs help moving the chicken coop. I didn't even know that was a thing?"

"It is! It prevents parasites from getting to the wood. It's also just healthy for the chickens to roam other areas of the farm, so moving it is important for them." I explain with my friends looking confused.

"Tanner, do you want to help?" Lucas asks with a nod.

"I'm a little too tipsy to be moving anything right now, dude." He answers back, before Lucas rolls his eyes and walks away.

Chelsea is quick to ask the question that I'm wondering, "Is there something going on between you two?"

"What? No." Tanner answers, looking between us, "You told her?" He looks at me with his brows contorted.

"Of course not!" I say, defending myself.

"It's very obvious." Chelsea says, squinting her eyes, "Or I'm just very good at knowing when a guy is gay."

Tanner shakes his head and chuckles, "Well, nothing is going on."

We look straight ahead, watching as Richard and Lucas meet in the middle of the field talking. It's interesting to see the two of them talking considering Richard was just talking about Lucas a few weeks ago, with jealousy lacing his tone. I didn't tell him Lucas was bisexual, but he seemed to let the animosity go as the two talked like it was all good.

Chelsea and I hum in response as we see Lucas look back at us for a quick moment. With the sun high in the sky, Chelsea excuses herself to grab her sunglasses. We ask her to bring back more alcohol and our own shades to protect our eyes.

"Okay, fine, something happened." Tanner says the moment Chelsea is out of earshot.

"Whaaaat?" I say trying to sound actually shocked, when it was fairly obvious that something happened between him and Lucas.

"Nice acting skills." He says, looking bored at me, "We kind of had a threesome the other night."

My mouth drops open. "And you were just going to pretend that everything was fine?"

"It wasn't my idea; it was Luke's. But my god, dude is stressed that I'm going to tell everyone. I'm only telling you because you're literally the only one that knows my problem with this, but you'd think he'd be the gay one with how much he's freaking out over it. We didn't even touch the entire time. We may have looked at each other once during the tower, but after that we haven't talked much since."

I put my drink in between my legs as I use my fingers to figure out the positioning of their threesome. Tanner looks down at my fingers and covers them.

"Stop that! He's going to see you!" He says quickly, "If he finds out that you know he's going to be pissed!"

I chuckle, "I'm sorry, but you had a threesome with a random woman and the guy you have a huge crush on. Right? So you have no one to blame but yourself for this one."

He gives me a look as he laughs and groans at the same time. "I hate myself."

"Are things that bad? You guys are best friends, right? It should be fine." Just then, Chelsea comes out with a full bottle of liquor and our sunglasses.

"What should be fine?" Chelsea asks as I slide on my glasses.

"Tanner thinks he fucked up his friendship with Lucas." I pause as I look over at him. "At least that's what I'm guessing from his facial expression."

"How am I supposed to deal with this?" Tanner asks as he twirls the sunglasses in his hands, "He thinks I'm straight, so I'm just supposed to pretend I didn't have a reaction to seeing him like that."

Chelsea frowns, "Oh, hon, you need better alcohol than vodka. I'll be right back." She leaves again to get a different type of alcohol. I smile lightly as she touches my shoulder while she walks back into the house.

"So I definitely didn't want to say this in front of her, but he's not straight either." I let the words slip from my mouth, hoping they land as delicately as my voice.

Tanner looks at me, "I'm sure you're just saying that to make me feel better, and while I appreciate that, I can't—"

"No, I mean, he literally told me he is bisexual, right around the time you told me that you were gay. And I wasn't supposed to tell you, but I'm ninety-nine percent sure that last night affected him too."

His eyelids drop. "Stop lying. Having a crush on him is already a problem. Throwing hope at me that he's gay and might be interested in me is just cruel."

I take a sip of my drink as Chelsea reappears with a new bottle. "You're right, what do I know? He's probably not thinking about you, naked with a girl on you..."

Tanner puts his glasses on just as I notice the red blush in his cheeks before he sits back in his seat and takes a large gulp of his drink.

"What are we watching here?" I ask, finally focusing on Richard and Lucas trying but failing to lift the chicken coop on their own.

"Normally, I would let this go on without getting involved, but I think one of us needs to offer our services." Chelsea says with a gesture towards Tanner. He points at himself, like he knows what she's talking about.

"Someone's gotta get me sober first." Tanner takes another sip of his drink. I roll my eyes at both of them before I get up from my spot on the swing.

"Where are you going?" Both of them say.

"I'm going to help them out." It takes me a little hike to make it to Lucas and Richard, but when I do, they're talking about the right way to lift and move the coop without hurting themselves. Lucas makes a joke about chicks and laughs, but Richard frowns.

"Speaking of chicks!" Luke says, letting out a forced laugh while pointing at me. Richard's head turns to look at me.

I gulp as I approach Richard, his eyes on me like a lion's on a gazelle. His jaw ticks as I come to Lucas' side and give him a quick side hug.

"You guys would have more luck with a crane, I think. Not that I doubt your abilities to lift a chicken coop; it's just—"

"We can do this. Can't we, Luke?" Richard's chin goes up as he looks at Lucas.

Lucas smiles, "Yeah, I'm sure it can't be that hard." Luke looks at me with 'help me' eyes.

"What if I get Graves to come help you both out?"

Richard's eyes bore into mine at the suggestion, "We don't need his help."

"I feel like you do though, and the more help, the easier it'll be to lift."

Richard's sigh through his nose makes me smirk, "No."

"If I could, I'd like to say we do need extra help." Lucas says in between us. "Maybe Ames can help us."

I shrug as I let my body language do the talking. "Yeah, Richard, let me help."

I watch my husband's eyes look down my body before his eyes settle on my lips.

I swallow, noticing his eyes flick down to my throat. "I'm going to get help." I say with a sigh, I leave before Richard tries to argue with me more.

Before I knew it, I convinced my sleeping brother to help his roommate and brother-in-law. I never thought I'd see the day of Graves and Richard working together, but maybe it's the fact that Lucas is there acting as a buffer, even if it's without his knowledge. The three of them begin to move the coop as Chelsea, Tanner, and I watch them as we get drunk. It felt like I had spent a good amount of time chatting and getting drunk with my friends, something I couldn't say I had earlier in the year. I felt like I was in true good company with both of them, even when we stopped laughing and got caught up watching the three guys pick up a heavy ass coop to move it over every ten feet.

"I hope I don't get smacked, but your brother is hot." Chelsea said before looking over at me and Tanner. I laugh out loud.

"Yeah, right. He's like the evil spawn of the family. I mean literally, he's got anger problems and has no filter."

"She's not wrong, though." Tanner says, looking at me.

"I know I'm not." I say with my brows furrowed.

"No. I mean, Graves is hot. Especially with his—" Tanner stops mid-sentence as his mouth hangs open. I look to see Chelsea with her mouth agape as well. When I face forward to see what they're staring at, I seem to understand why they made those faces. As my brother, Lucas and Richard are carrying the coop with no shirts on. We're a decent distance away from them, but I can still see my husband's muscles work as his veins bulge.

"Wow." The three of us say in unison.

"Is it possible that I'm pregnant?" Tanner asks first.

"Only if that means I'm in labor, because my water definitely just broke." Chelsea answers jokingly.

"Okay, ew." I squint as I look at her, "That's my brother you're talking about."

"Look! I mean, just look at them!" She says, using her hands to gesture to them. "They are men, built like gods, and we're just puny women that they can man-handle and can just take us—"

"Chelsea!" I say seriously but can't stop the smile that spreads on my face.

"You try online dating, and then we can talk." She sighs, "He's just so—"

I roll my eyes at her and look over at Tanner, who looks ready to crawl out of his skin.

"I need to go inside for a bit," Tanner says before he gets up and disappears.

"You think that was because he needed to handle himself?" Chelsea asks, winking at me.

"Oh my god, you need to get laid!"

"I know! Put in a good word for me?" She says with a smile.

"A good word with who? Graves? Are you crazy?" I say it loud enough that I don't realize the shock on her face until I turn and see my brother in front of us with no shirt on.

"You call for me?" Graves asks as he uses his shirt to wipe sweat from his head and then chest.

"Yeah. Put your shirt back on, you tool." I shake my head at him, though most of it is geared towards Chelsea, especially when she whimpers as he puts his shirt back on.

"You feel better about that?" He asks with a grin as the sun shines in his face.

"Yeah, but you're still being weird. Go away." I say as he looks between me and Chelsea before he heads back in the house.

Chelsea groans as she falls back into the seat, causing us to swing. I have to hold onto my cup from sloshing all over the place. Lucas and Richard walk up to us next as Chelsea keeps pretending to cry in an obvious way.

"What's wrong with her?" Lucas asks with a frown, feeding her attention to do it more.

"Nothing. Tanner is inside if you were wondering." I say through a petty smile.

Luke's frown shifts into a look of guilt as he gulps, "Right. Thanks?"

Richard's eyes shift from Chelsea to me and then the barn. I look over at my friend, who grabs her drink and starts chugging it.

"Are you going to be okay if I disappear for a bit?" I ask Chelsea with a small wince.

She looks at me for a moment before I watch her eyesight focus on Richard. I don't know what she thinks is going to happen, but I can see her gears turning.

"I'm okay living in misery; I've been doing it for six months now. Go and have hot sex with your husband." She says it loud enough that my cheeks heat. It's enough for me to know that Richard and I should not have any alone time when my drunk friend seems to need me, even if she's being overdramatic about it. I pat her shoulder before I walk over to Richard, stopping a few steps away from him. Almost like we both know what would happen if we touched, especially with his chest on display.

Richard's jaw tenses as I open my mouth and close it as the rest of his muscles ripple in the sunlight.

"We probably shouldn't be talking right now." I wince at my own words, though Richard doesn't seem to react, only letting his head tilt to the side for a moment.

"You're probably right." He clears his throat as he closes some space between us. "Wouldn't want you to have sex with your husband." Richard whispers in my ear. "God forbid I put you over my shoulder and take you to the stables to fuck you on top of a haybale."

Heat rises to my cheeks as I feel warmth drip between my legs. I look at my husband just as the corners of his lips upturn for a second. Evil, my sweaty husband is evil for the teasing words that escaped his mouth. A full sentence I'd never imagined came from Richard's lips, but the temptation to follow him is great as he doesn't give me a chance to respond and just walks to the stables by himself.

I force my jaw to come back together before a bug can fly in, as I look back at Chelsea, who's got the biggest grin on her face. The little liar, how did she become such a close friend for someone who teases, picks and prods, and manages to lie straight to my face? She pats the space next to her on the swing. I shake my head at her. I can't believe I fell for her little trick.

Since being back on the farm, I didn't notice the time that flew by, there had been so many great days and so many bad ones that they had blurred together. It had felt like a lifetime ago since I had packed up my stuff and moved out from Florida. My life had changed significantly.

Tanner brought the scale over to me as I stepped on it, reading the results. My weight had dropped, I was forty pounds lighter. It had been a few months since the training started. Lucas had gotten me into a calorie deficit diet, Tanner had trained me at their gym, even the therapy helped me. Not to mention working on the farm had kept me busy, on the off chance I wasn't doing that, Chelsea had even invited me to a couple of her dance classes. Chelsea's dance classes were pole dancing classes, and never did I think I'd ever see myself, a big fat girl on a pole, but after the first three sessions, I really loved doing it.

I had plenty of hobbies and things to occupy my brain. Even after all of it, my thoughts would go to Richard. While Richard had been a popular topic in therapy, there were more important topics that took center stage. I couldn't for the life of me understand what my therapist had asked of me until she spelled it out.

"Tell him. All of it. He needs to hear it from you." My therapist's gorgeous voice rang in my head. It continued to ring as Richard approached me. He was walking towards me with no shirt on again. I hummed, trying to avoid looking at his muscles, but damn did he make it hard.

"You have some food on your face there." Richard said, bending to wipe it off with his thumb. Ready to slap him for it, I watched as he slid his thumb into his mouth. My restraint was better than ever for not reacting to him by licking and sucking the tip of his thumb.

151

"Thanks." I said back, blinking, before I looked down at my chicken salad sandwich. I looked back up to see my husband daring to sit next to me.

"Hope you don't mind, I need the break. It's really hot today."

My mouth tugged up, "I'm sure you need a break right next to me, right?"

"Best seat in the house is right next to my wife."

I let my head lean to the side, "You really want that to work, huh? Do you really think all of this is going to win me over?" I asked, waving my hand towards the farm, towards all the work he's done for my parents and me.

"What do you want me to do? Tell me and I'll do it."

"Tell you?" I scoffed, "You really want me to tell you?"

"Yes. Tell me everything, Amelia. I'm not here to win you over, I'm here to fix whatever I did that made you leave in the first place. You know I love you." Richard says with his eyebrows rising and falling.

"We lost the baby, Ramsey." I've imagined saying these words out loud a thousand times, I've imagined breaking down when I said them, but when I say them with such anger, it doesn't seem like the words hold meaning.

I watch as Richard's expression retreats. His smile drops, and his scowl appears.

"I lost the baby in my belly, and for three weeks we acted like we were going to be okay, that we'd try again when I was better."

"Amelia."

"It's been a year, a little over if my memory has anything to say about it. And it does, because I relive that pain every damn day. I can't get up some mornings because I remember that our daughter would've been in our world with us."

"Turtle, please."

"No." I smack his hand away, "This is what I'm talking about. And this is only part of it. I was your everything, and those weeks were the closest we've ever been in such a long time. But now? Now you're just the memory of the man I used to know. I don't even think you're the same man anymore."

"Please, Amelia. I haven't—"

"Did you even hear what people said when I came to visit you?"

I watch as Richard's eyes look down no longer at me, because he knows I know.

"Do you think I haven't heard the crap spewed about me? *'How could she end up with him? How do you think Ramsey has sex with his fat wife? She must be a gold digger. She must have a serious problem for him to marry her.*"

"You honestly think I give a crap about what the random fangirls say?"

"Do you honestly think they're the only ones? What about Capsley? What about Hughes? What about any other guy on your team?"

"What they think doesn't matter."

"Have you even defended me? Have you ever told them to stop when they call me fat behind my back? Did you ever care to try and make an effort for me?"

Richard lets out the longest sigh I've ever heard as I wait for him to answer. He shakes his head as if that's good enough. Maybe he expects me to say more, or maybe he's stewing on his next response, but either way, I feel it in my gut.

MIKA C.C.

"This is over, Richard. You've changed, and you don't even see it." I show him my empty ring finger, "See this? I don't even wear my ring, and you still don't get it. We can't keep doing this, this thing we're doing. Please understand when I say it... We need to get a divorce."

Chapter Twenty

Richard – Past

AMELIA (18), RICHARD (20)

I had only driven around my hometown once since starting college and it had been to see Amelia. Us living so far apart has been an adjustment, being back for winter vacation made it better though.

There were not many places in our town that needed cars. The exception was living thirty minutes away from my university in the city. Even when I'd walk from my house to Amelia's it always seemed like a trek. In the past when I wanted the car there was little to no hope with my older siblings stealing it out from under me, this day was different.

My parents were quick to get me out of the house, as weird as it had been, I took the opportunity before it could slip away. I hadn't called, but I had just assumed it would be okay, it always had been in the past.

The moment I parked the car, I knew something was wrong, the air felt charged, and the animals didn't make a sound. After three knocks on the door, Amelia's mom answered.

"Oh. Hi Ramsey. Amelia isn't feeling great right now." Her mom's voice sounded sad, almost like she'd been crying.

"Is she sick?"

Her mom blinked, "Why don't you talk to Graves? Hmm?" She led me inside the house, where even inside seemed quieter. The animal clock in the kitchen barely ticked as the seconds went by, the living room that was always lively every other time I had come was empty and soundless. Tranquil was not the word I would've used for the feeling that surrounded me.

Graves exited his room with his mom, just barely making eye contact with me. Whatever had happened was more than just a little bad news.

"Hey." His monotonous voice didn't exactly convince me he was okay either, but still I asked.

"You okay?" Both of us watched as his mom walked past us until she was in her room.

"What is going on? Where is Amelia?" My questions coming out a lot faster now that his mom isn't present.

"She's dead..." My eyes grew wide with his answer.

"Amelia?"

Graves looks at me with a scowl, "No, Calliope. Amelia had just come back in from brushing her, and when we looked to make sure the horses were all accounted for, we just saw her... laying in the grass."

The shock on my face didn't leave, "And you're sure she was—"

He nods, "We even had the vet come out, he and his team took her to the crematorium for us."

"I'm so sorry, Graves." My voice cracks just imagining how Amelia must feel. I watch Graves shake his head as he turns to head back for his room.

"I knew I hated horses." He mumbled just loud enough for me to still hear. I could only hope it was his grief talking. "Amelia is on the roof... Not this one, but the horse's stables. That's where you can find her."

After racing through Amelia's parents house, I nearly ran to the stables, the news of Callie still reeling in my mind. Never again would I see Amelia ride her favorite horse, never would I either. I'd never get that moment of pure friendship from a horse that came from such a bad place. Amelia had called me the horse whisperer because of my connection with Calliope. Now it was gone...

"How'd you find me?" Amelia had the nerve to ask as I was two steps away from joining her on the roof.

"Graves." My short answer just made her scoff.

"I hate him. I hate this. This has to be a dream, a really bad one." A sniffle following her sentence, "I loved her."

"Me too." I said, sitting next to Amelia, who was laying on the roof, just looking at the stars.

The silence between us wasn't hard or heavy, just the kind of silence that I imagined death would be.

"What can I do?" I asked before I really thought of it. I studied her as she turned her head to look at me.

"What can you do, what can you do? Can you bring her back? Can you tell me that she's in a better place? Can you tell me why? Can you? Why is this happening now?"

Amelia's words nearly broke me, every question she asked had no answer, except maybe one, but even I didn't feel right answering it for her. Instead, I wrapped my arms around her and let her cry. I couldn't stand that I didn't have the answers she wanted, I hated that I couldn't do more for her.

I had planned a life with that horse, Calliope was to thank for most of my life with Amelia. She had been the reason I talked to her for the first time, Callie had essentially been my wing-horse. She helped me get my first kiss, my first girlfriend and my first love. Even when it came to both of our first times having sex, it felt like Calliope pushed us into it. Mostly because she literally pushed me on top of Amelia while I was playing with the horse.

"Will you stay with me, Rooster?"

I exhaled a shaky breath, "Of course, Turtle."

"So if we ever get married and I get fat, you promise to never leave me and to always stick up for me if I get teased?" Her question caught me off guard, I almost laughed at it, but I know she's serious. My girlfriend has always thought about the worst-case scenario, and just hearing Amelia talk about it right after what happened to Callie... I couldn't help but answer her, just to stay off the topic of our favorite horse.

"Of course. No one would dare to tease my wife, though, and if they did, I'd kill them."

Amelia chuckled, nuzzling her head further into me. "You'll stay with me now, then?"

"Now and forever." I mumbled under my breath.

She hummed in question.

"I'm not going anywhere, Amelia."

From there we talked about our future, where we saw ourselves, parts of ourselves I don't remember sharing with her before. Both of us cuddled under the stars as we stared into the night sky, the night air just barely breezing by us, and the quiet noise of crickets filling in the noise. Our conversations went deeper, became more real, as we shared our deepest fears.

For the first time, I felt closer to Amelia than I'd ever known her before. And again, it was all thanks to Calliope. The eternal thank you I'd have for the horse would be stuck in every memory I had of Amelia, my girlfriend, my fiance, my future wife. There wasn't anything that would stop me from loving this woman for the rest of my life, and as I said it, I remembered the last words I said to Calliope.

On one of the first rides I ever had on the horse, I remembered saying the exact same words. The memory of kissing Amelia while I rode Calliope, to the last time I saw Callie...

"I'll take good care of her, Callie. Don't you worry about that. Amelia is my world."

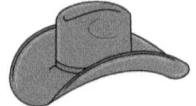

Chapter Twenty-One

Richard – Present

I don't move when I hear Amelia's footsteps; I close my eyes and pretend like I'm sleeping. Being on the roof of the horse's stables was her thing. Maybe she needed it, but I needed it too. I don't even budge when I feel her presence come close to me. I know she settles close by me, and I try not to say anything. The things I want to say are too heavy, too real and I'm not ready to be that vulnerable.

A deep breath is all I take without needing to open my eyes. My hands behind my head as my pillow, I could fall asleep like this—with her next to me; it's been hard to sleep as it is. Sleeping without my wife next to me is something I never wished for. Amelia cuddling next to me all of a sudden feels new as my body manages to freeze at the contact of her body so close to mine. We're not fucking, we're not arguing, so this closeness feels awkward and undeserving.

I don't say anything, instead letting us lay in silence. The air is dry, but the space between us feels clammy. Everything about the way she feels against me should be right, but even I know it feels wrong. Even

I can tell that no matter what has happened in the last few days, we haven't gotten over whatever this is.

"Can you just tell me why you couldn't say anything?" Amelia's voice comes out so soft; it's how I know she's imagined asking the question a million times, but when it came down to it, she waited until it took up so much space in her mind that she couldn't even blow up at me.

The hard breath I exhale sounds like I'm annoyed, but I hope she knows I'm trying to figure out the right words to say so that she understands it's not on her...

"Richard." I feel her pull her head off my arm, and that's when I decide to open my eyes and look at the woman whose eyes are glistening, waiting for anything to come out of my mouth. The way her chest caves like she's about to start crying if I don't answer, I know what'll come even if I do respond and tell her everything.

"I fucked up." I respond before the first tear falls from her face, "I can't have you looking at me like this if you want to hear this. So could you please lay back down? On me, or the roof."

She bites her bottom lip before complying to lay back down next to me, not exactly cuddled up like before, but close enough to feel her warmth. There's a second of silence where both of us sigh as we get comfortable with what's about to come out of my mouth.

"I should've fought. I should've said more. I didn't realize at the time that not saying anything would do more harm than good, Amelia. You have to believe that. I don't know where it started, when it bugged you, or even when it bugged me. But it did. It truly broke me up to know that people were talking badly about you. I know you know that I grew up in the eyes of our town, so once I was in the majors with Roman as my agent, it wasn't all that different. But I didn't know it was going to come with more rules. I couldn't get into fights; I couldn't raise my voice. I couldn't put myself in a position that would get me in trouble. I watched it happen with Graves, and he almost lost his spot. I even watched it almost happen to players on my team. I loved the game so much I didn't realize not speaking up, not standing up for you was going to be our problem."

I take a pause and finally turn to look at her, my wife, silently crying next to me. I can't help but wipe them away. I thought I'd always be the one to stop her from crying, not the reason for her tears. I had promised myself that the last time we were up on this roof together.

"I was stupid; I fucked everything up because I let the game get in my head when I should've put you first. You were right; I put the game first instead of defending the woman I love. The woman I never wanted to make cry, the woman that I'm absolutely obsessed with. You leaving me was a wake-up call. That's why I can't stay away; that's why I can't leave, because not only are you my wife, but without you, baseball doesn't make sense. Without you, I have no other purpose. The days you weren't with me in Florida, I coasted, my streak broke, and I realized there was no point to baseball without you by my side. I know it sounds ridiculous, but you're right, baseball doesn't matter. The house in Florida doesn't matter."

With my hand on her face, I feel her breaths get ragged the more I talk.

"I understand it all now, and I'm sorry for not realizing how much you mattered back then, but I'm here now, and I'm fighting like hell to prove to you that nothing else matters. Dammit, you're the only thing that matters in my life. I swear if I lose—" My words get cut off by Amelia's soft lips on mine; the curves of her body fit into me as I push my lips further into hers. It's not until she straddles me that I finally feel all of her. My hands make no time to feel every part of her body that I love; it's everywhere. Her arms, her breasts, her stomach, her thighs and her waist, her back and that ass—I touch everywhere I can before we're taking off our clothes.

We waste no time, but I can't fuck her without tasting her. When my tongue darts out to lick her cunt, I can't help but moan at the taste of her sweet pussy. Amelia shushes me, but I press my tongue deeper into her until she lets out a moan herself. I look up at her as I continue lapping her until I feel her body tense under my mouth and hands. I only come up to try and ask her what this is—what we're doing is right—but before I do, our mouths crash against each other. The tip of my dick presses into her wetness, and even though a part of me questions all of it, I slide into her with ease. Both of us made noises with horses below us and the rest of the farm to hear us. When I'm inside of Amelia, I can't stop. Add it to my list of addictions she's given me; her love, her kisses, her warmth, her pussy and fucking her are addictions I never want to get rid of. I never want to stop coming inside of her. I never want to stop loving her. Every part of her swallows me whole until I feel my cum seep into her; even with my dick limp, I don't stop pumping until I feel her pussy clench and feel our cum stir together with both of us attached.

Amelia looks up at me like we've just made love, but I know that can't be it. I know there's still a million things we haven't said. It's not that I don't believe us fucking could bring us back together; it's that she's only just let me speak for me to know that we won't be together until we've talked about everything.

163

MIKA C.C.

By the time both of us are dressed, dread has crept back up into my throat, the way both of us don't bother speaking a word about what just happened. Like it was a momentary lapse, like it was just us reacting to each other; is this what it would be like if we divorced and still saw each other? Would we pretend like nothing happened for just a few minutes and fuck like it was just us all over again?

"Amelia."

She looks at me hesitantly, with a look she saves just for me.

"Nothing's changing, is it? No matter how many times we argue, no matter what I say, or how many times we do this?" I use my finger to point at both of us.

She bites her lip. "Remember the last time we were up here?"

"Kind of hard to forget that."

"I feel like this might be the place where we will always grieve our losses."

I took a sharp breath. "So that's what this was—grieving our loss of our marriage?"

Amelia shrugs as she lets her arms fall at her sides with a slap. "I don't know. I'm trying here. We're just in two different places. I'm trying to get over you, but your being here reminds me of how I fell in love with you. And you're here trying to win me back, so how am I supposed to react when you say the things that could fix everything, even after you've broken my heart?"

I clench my teeth together; there's not much I can say when what she asks is rhetorical. The sounds of the crickets singing are all we get when I walk up to her, eating the space between us. I'm not sure what the right move is, but not being next to her, not touching her—all of it overwhelms me.

"You can grieve me all you want; you can grieve what we had, that I understand... But I don't want to lose you. We can start over, start fresh, not forgetting but just trying to move forward together."

"I don't think I can do that, Richard. It's too hard, especially when I look at you and still see the man that didn't say anything." Amelia says as she leans into my hand as I brush my knuckles against her cheek.

"I'll prove to you I'm not that same man anymore. You need to know that I'm not that guy; I can't lose you. Amelia, you have every piece of my heart—"

"Richard—" I shut her up with my lips, her hands finding my shirt, gripping the fabric tightly as our tongues dance. She only separates us to say my name again before I push my lips back into hers.

"I can't give up this feeling." I say when we separate again, my cock pulsing between us.

"We're going to keep circling like this if we don't stop." Amelia says, sounding out of breath.

"Do you want to stop? You can tell me no, and I'll respect that."

"Saying no seems like the right thing to do—but right now I don't want to be right." Our lips come back together like it's the only thing keeping us together, like air isn't our form of oxygen but our breaths are. We make out until both of us are lying back down on the roof, Amelia grinding her pussy over my cock. We're like teens humping until both of us pull down our pants again, begging for that reconnection. I expect her to slide herself on top of me. I'm panting as my calloused fingers graze over her soft skin, as she teases her pussy against the tip of my cock, until she comes off, her lips kiss down my neck, passing my covered chest. She pulls the bottom of my shirt up; my cock twitches with her face so close.

MIKA C.C.

Amelia looks at me like I should know what comes next. The way her eyes look under the stars gives me a hint, but before I can think too much of it, her mouth wraps around my dick. The breath I suck in isn't enough air as her mouth goes further down. I can only groan so loud in the night with her sucking my cock like it's the best thing she's ever tasted. My hands tangle in her hair as she sucks me harder with both hands wrapped around me. She's never been able to take me fully down her throat, but she tries with her hands guiding her, with my hands in her hair slowing her down. Amelia looks up at me as she gags, her mouth opening just enough to lick me from the base to my tip. She pulls my shirt up more as her tongue licks up my chest, until her tongue can't lick anymore skin. My hand grabs her neck lightly as I bring her lips back to mine, both of us moaning at the taste of her and my dick on my tongue. I let go of her neck long enough for Amelia to sink her pussy on top of me, my cock harder than ever, wet with her saliva as I fill up her pussy.

"Neither of us are going to stop this, are we?" Amelia asks as she arches her back to fuck me.

"Fuck, not when it feels this good." I answer as she pushes me further into her, both of us moaning.

"That's what I thought." She bends to kiss me as the slaps of our skin just make us want each other more, making me realize that what we're doing is making things more complicated than it is fixing our relationship.

166

The word divorce rings in my ears more than ever. The sentence falling from my wife's lips is even more disturbing as I hear her voice repeat it over and over again. No matter how long I stay in her parents house, no matter how much time I put in to convince her I'm not that man, she still sees me as him. As the asshole, the jerk, the massive douchebag that can't even stand up for his wife.

Amelia's right, I deserved it, I deserved every bit of what she said to me. I deserved to hear how she felt about our baby that didn't make it. If my wife had known the tears I shed over our loss, she'd maybe feel differently, but I can't help myself. Amelia's made herself clear on what she wants. And it's not me...

My therapist told me that in order to move on, I have to apologize. She told me my depression wins if I don't do the big things that matter. I was never a full believer in therapy, but the moment Amelia said the 'd' word, I knew I had to speak to someone. I called the first doctor I found on the internet and have had three sessions since.

As much as I gave Amelia space, every part of me said not to, not only because of my therapist, but because I missed her. Physically, mentally and any other way I could have her, I had spent most of my life with Amelia. I couldn't walk away from that. Add in my morning duties on the farm, seeing Amelia sit down outside enjoying a book with her coffee was a morning ritual within itself.

I spent another morning watching her as I carried hay to the horses stables, it wasn't until she looked up that I turned my head and got back to work. By the time I made it back to her parents house, magically without speaking a word to my wife, her dad was sitting at the dining table, looking oddly like he'd been waiting for me. Amelia's mom gave me a small smile, asking me to sit with them...

"I don't know how else to start this other than by saying, we're going on vacation." Amelia's dad, Dante, said the moment I sat across from him.

"That's great. You two deserve to get away." I am not exactly sure why I feel so awkward sitting with my in-laws. "Why do you guys look sad though?"

"Amelia told us what happened." Amelia's mom says with a frown, "You can stay here while we're gone, maybe you can take care of Bear for us? But when we get back from our trip... You'll have to find a new place to stay."

I hold in a breath before I answer, "Of course. Makes sense." I purse my lips before looking down at the table, even my in-laws are getting rid of me.

"Hey, Mags, can you get us some coffee?" Dante asks his wife, "From the little shop down the road?"

"Oh. Sure. I'll let you boys work out the details..." Maggie says before disappearing out the front door. Her husband waits until we hear the truck start before he speaks.

"What can I do to help you and Amelia get back together?"

I look at my father-in-law with wide eyes, thinking he couldn't be serious. The thought that this couldn't be my reality hit me square in the face. No, that was Amelia's dad, his expression seeming even more sincere than his question.

"Just tell me what to say to my daughter. I don't usually get involved in your business, but I know she's going to regret her decision if you two truly get divorced. She still talks about you like she's in love with you, Junior. If you have a plan, now's the time to rope me in, before our flight if at all possible." Her dad says with a small smile, reminding me of Amelia's smile.

There had been no plan, even with Amelia's dad trying to help me come up with one, there was no point. The only thing I could do is tell her how I feel, and that wasn't a plan. That wasn't what she wanted to hear. I should've heard Amelia from the beginning, the time apart, then the note about the separation, and now divorce...

Had she really fallen out of love with me, as I tried to show her I was worth staying for? Had I been that blind and deaf not to listen to her, even though she told me she loved me? Or was I making her tell me what I wanted to hear? Was all of this my fault, for pushing her to be around me, for showing her what she meant to me? Maybe these were the questions I should've talked to my therapist about, instead, I drove over to the farm.

Amelia's the one to open the door the moment I knock on the door, her dark hair flying behind her from the movement of the door. I get a waft of her perfume, and it makes me want to greet her with an embrace so I could bury myself in her scent, in that signature perfume that hooked me from the beginning.

"Richard." She blinked, "What are you doing here?"

"You told me everything, right?"

"I did." Amelia's breath hitches, as she moves out of the entryway, "Come in." It only feels right since I was invited in, but even as I enter her house, I feel my hands shake with the thought that everything might fall apart.

"Did I make you say anything you didn't want to? Did I do all of this just to make you feel bad for me? Did I make you feel vulnerable and not like yourself?"

"Richard, I don't think this is helpful..."

My head shakes slightly, "Maybe not, but I need to know I'm not crazy. That what we've been doing the last few weeks has been real and not just you leading me on. Were any of the things you said to me true?"

I watch as the beautiful hazel eyes I've stared at for most of my life, change into a color I've never seen as they fill with tears. I want to assume I know what those tears mean, that she regrets everything... I turn, ready to leave her house, but she grabs my forearm before I get to the door. I look back at Amelia as she tries to hold back her tears from falling.

"Do you know how hard it is not loving you? Do you know how much I regret saying everything? The idea of divorcing... I've been in love with you since I was twelve. That'll never go away. Even when I thought we'd do better with other people... You deserve someone who can give you what you want, the same way I deserve someone who can put me first." She says before swallowing.

"Amelia, there's no one else who can give me what I want, because no one even comes close to you. You are the only someone that can give me what I want."

"B-but..."

"There's no buts, Turtle. You're it for me. There's nothing for me back in Florida. I sent in my official notice of retirement weeks ago. The last of it is up to you. I'll sign the paper if that's what you need to be happy, but there's only one way for me to be happy. I'm not telling you this to convince you to stay with me. I'm saying it because if I don't, then what was this all for?"

Amelia looks at me with a waterfall of tears down her face, I'm not even sure she knows what she does to me when she cries like that. If she knows that I'm holding every part of myself together, to not cry with her, to not hold her and tell her to stay, to stay with me and love me for the rest of our lives.

The longer we stand in her foyer with Amelia crying and my questions left hanging in the air, just disconnects us more. I turn to head to the door, but before I'm able to get my hand on the doorknob, Amelia steps between me and the door.

My brows crease, wondering what she's going to say as she opens her mouth, but nothing but air comes out. Amelia's lips shut like she's fighting the urge to say what she needs to. I move closer to her just so I can open the door, but as I do, her arms wrap around me as her lips crash into mine. My hand loosens from the doorknob as her tongue presses against the seam of my lips. My lips stay sealed as she removes her lips from mine.

"Richard." Her eyes glisten, "I don't want anyone else, I don't want to go through life without you. I don't want a divorce, I just want the man I fell in love with back."

"I'm right here. I'm right here, Turtle." I press my lips back to Amelia's, wishing they could tell her my story. Our mouths opened for each other as my arms wrapped around her. I feel her tug my hair as I push her against the door, our tongues dancing deeper into each other's mouths. I grab Amelia's hips just to walk her closed bedroom door, her back hits the door as her hand escapes my hand to find the door. While the door swings open, I press her into the threshold, our bodies melting into each other as we continue to make out.

All of this to prove my point, that neither of us can be without each other. I can't resist my wife. I can't live without my first love.

Chapter Twenty-Two

Amelia – Present

"Richard..." I whisper as he pins me to the threshold to my bedroom.

"Tell me to stop." He says as his hand slides up my dress, "C'mon little Turtle, tell me to stop." Richard whispers as I feel his fingers reach the edge of my underwear. I feel his fingers fight with the elastic.

Just as I open my eyes, Richard's blue eyes lock on mine, "Oh god." It's the last word to leave my lips as I feel one of his fingers plunge into my core. I freeze as I feel him inside of me, his finger curling and pumping slowly.

"Do you want me to stop now?" Richard asks as his finger continues. I watch him as his head dips down to kiss my shoulder.

I shake my head as I feel a moan rise out of me. "No. God, don't stop." I try not to get lost in the little kisses he leaves across my shoulder and collarbone.

He reaches my neck, kissing until he reaches my ear, "Do you want me to take you to your bed? I could play with your clit, lick you until you've left my face sopping wet. Or I could fuck you with my fingers right here until you're begging for my cock."

"Shit, Richard." I moan as I feel him enter a second finger.

"I need *my wife* to tell me what she wants. I need her to tell me, right fucking now." Richard says as he sucks my earlobe into his mouth as he breathes into my ear, creating goosebumps across my entire body. Nothing interests me more, I've never wanted another man before him, and I'm not sure any man could ever compare to him. I'd fought him so much in the last three months he'd been here, but I couldn't anymore. Not with his fingers inside me, not with the memories of every night and day we've spent tangled up in sheets together. The tension we had since he ate me out in the truck had permanently altered me. Not with every word ringing in my head.

"Take me, Ramsey." I felt his mouth remove from my skin as he brought himself to look at me, "Take me to bed right fucking now." I swear I could see a sheen in my husband's eyes I hadn't seen in a long while. The moment he blinks, the shine disappears and his eyes darken. Richard's fingers slid out of me, leaving me feeling empty and dry, but he quickly hoisted me up around his waist and walked me into my room. I closed the door the moment we were far enough in, if we stalled any longer, the moment would pass. I could feel the reluctance creeping in as Richard set me on the bed. Even though I had nearly slammed the door from being in his arms, he walked back to lock it.

The air felt thick the moment Richard looked at me with a need rising in his jeans. I could look at him all day, especially with the look he had on his face, as if he worshiped me, as if I were the only woman in the entire world. It had been so long since he looked at me that way, I couldn't even remember the last time Richard looked at me that way. I wanted to cry just trying to remember it, I closed my eyes tightly for a moment just to stop the inevitable. I didn't want to cry in this moment, not when I wanted him so fucking badly. Not when I could see his cock bulging out of his pants. When I opened my eyes, I expected to see Richard getting undressed or doing something to prepare us for sex. Instead, what I saw made me stand up immediately.

Chapter
Twenty-Three

Richard – Present

I'd barely unbuttoned my jeans when Amelia closed her eyes. The moment she did, I lost it. I'm not sure where it even came from, maybe from the tension that had been rising between us, it'd been like falling in love with her all over again. But I knew that expression on her face, I knew I'd hurt her in the past, and this was her pushing it down, trying to forget it. It'd been like the day she found out Callie died. Amelia had forgotten I knew her. I knew her facial expressions, I knew her body. I knew every piece of her, and I'd have every part of her memorized until my death bed. I could tell her exactly what she was feeling, even if she didn't want to talk about it.

"Ramsey?" My name from her mouth came out so softly, it nearly made me lose it all over again, "Richard?" I hardly registered the noise of her bedsheet, her body in the hazy blur of my tears. Amelia wrapped her arms around me and tried to shush me, I'm not sure how we both ended up on the bed with my head on her chest as she held me. I should've taken note when she brought my head up to look at her, in her crystalized eyes with wet cheeks.

I wiped my thumb across her cheek as she had been wiping away my tears for the last hour and a half. "Amelia, I am so sorry." I stopped myself from letting a croak out of my throat, "I'm so sorry for everything. I should've tried harder. I should've been better. I should've done more. I know I'd been an asshole. I knew what I was doing, and I didn't think—"

"Richard, you've already explained this to me."

"No. It's not enough, it'll never be. I don't deserve this. I know you're trying to forget all the moments I've fucked up, I know you're pretending to want me. No matter what I say, I know it'll never get you to fully forgive me, and I don't blame you. You shouldn't take me back." I couldn't even tell if tears fell as I spoke, my face felt numb.

"Richard, stop." Amelia says with a hard grip of both of her hands on the sides of my face, proving I still had feeling, at least when she touched me.

"I've seen the pain on your face, Amelia, how am I supposed to stop?" My voice breaks at the end of my sentence. "How am I supposed to be okay with breaking your heart?"

"You're not. You're not going to stop, you're not going to forget these things. Just like I'm not going to either."

"Exactly, Amelia." I say as I look into her eyes, "There's nothing that we can do to fix it."

"Yes, there is." Amelia's eyes fill with water, "Dammit, Richard. There is. I've seen it."

"What do you mean?" I ask as I anxiously bite my lip.

"There's always a way to fix a broken heart. And I know I'm going to sound super cliche and cheesy saying it. But I know it because the last couple weeks, I've experienced it. You've been putting my broken heart back together, and you never realized it."

"I don't think that's possible, Turtle."

"If it were impossible, you wouldn't be here, *Rooster*. All the little things add up. The night at the club? The barn. Hell, the other day on the truck."

"That was just lust—"

"No, Richard. It wasn't just lust, it was us. I don't line dance with anyone else. I don't stay up late looking at the stars, talking about stupid shit with just anyone. I don't just have sex with anyone in the stables. I don't ever get trapped in a mud pit with a four-wheel drive truck." She answers with a smirk on her lips.

"In my defense, I'd thought your brother invested in an all-wheel drive truck." I said with a bit of annoyance in my tone, though I see the playful look in her eyes when she looks back at me.

"My brother is not farm smart like I am." Amelia says like the true cowgirl she is.

I sighed, "It still doesn't change that I fucked everything up."

"You're right. It doesn't." Amelia responds with her own sigh, "You know what it does mean though?"

"What's that?"

"That you've had to work twice as hard to put everything back."

"I don't feel like I have." I feel my heartbeat quicken, like my throat might close up from speaking the truth.

"You have. And you're still doing it. We could've been having sex right now, but instead we're doing this."

I bite my lip as I look at her, "As true as that is, I have no right to your body. No matter how long we've been together and how well we've known each other. I have no claim on you, I lack the privilege to touch you."

I watch one of Amelia's brows raise, "Richard, you've never needed me to tell you this, but just this once I will." I manage to stay as still as possible as Amelia puts her hands on my shoulders and scoots her body closer to me, until both legs straddle me on the bed. I watch her take a long, deep breath, as I notice her eyes dip to my lips. I can feel my body tighten as I resist the urge to grab her thick thighs, I don't want to imagine a world without touching Amelia. I've told her a million times before, but I'll never tire of telling her. I open my mouth to say the words again but her hand covers my mouth.

"I don't want you to say anything else." Amelia says with a rasp in her voice. "I want you to touch me, Richard. I want to feel you inside me. I want your hands on me, I know you've gotten mixed signals from me before, but let me be as clear as day. I've never not wanted you to touch me, Richard. I will always want you, my husband, my best friend, to touch me wherever you want, whenever you see fit. This isn't just a want, Richard, it's a need. It's been my number one need from the moment we met." Amelia slowly removes her hand from my mouth as our eyes stay locked together.

"Do you mean that? Do you really need my touch? Because I can't live without it, Amelia. I didn't even know how much it meant to me until you were gone. You have no idea how badly I missed it, how badly

I missed this." I let my hands and fingers draw up her legs. "Tasting you, teasing you, touching you, is my beginning, middle and end."

"Richard." I can't stop looking into Amelia's eyes to make sure she's okay with everything I do. I'll never go back to the man I was, if it means always keeping my eyes on her.

"I'm done waiting, Amelia. Are you?"

She nods, "Yes. I'm done, I'm done with keeping myself away from you when I need you." Our mouths crash together in a fast movement, but we take it slow, letting our tongues sink together. I feel Amelia's hands on my shoulders slide down my chest as mine travel up until each of my palms hold her face. I pull back for just a moment and look at her.

"What?" Amelia asks, already out of breath.

"You're just perfect. In every single way." I say quickly before her hands cup my cheeks and she kisses me.

"I believe you, but please, I need you." Amelia says while grazing herself on top of me. I can't feel much under my pants except the steady heat coming from her.

"I know. I need you too, Turtle." I let my hands explore her body until I reach the hem of her dress and start to pull it off. Amelia's arms go up just to help me take it off her, and the moment I do, her breasts bounce, in a very thin garment I'd never even call a bra, not with its lack of support, especially with it showing me her nipples. I don't even bother to take it off, not when I go for her lips first. I kiss her, letting my tongue linger in her mouth for a minute before I kiss her chin down to her jawline, to that little spot near her ear she loves, then to her neck. I can hear her every breath, feel her chest underneath my lips as I make my way to her breasts, kissing them through the fabric, sucking her nipple in my mouth, as I listen to my wife moan my name.

I wait until I think her breath evens out and I suck in her other nipple, grazing it with my teeth as my tongue flicks back and forth. Amelia's breath picks up again as I feed my hand through her underwear and play with her clit. I feel her wetness with another finger but focus solely on her clit as my tongue plays with her breasts. Amelia's hands go for my arms, my hair, and my shirt until she can't hold onto me anymore. I look up at her with her eyes shut tight as I play with her, waiting for her release. Amelia's mouth opens slightly before she bites her lower lip, the look that I know as she's about to come for me. As I keep my pace with my finger circling in slow, deliberate counter-clockwise movements. Amelia's hands grab back onto me just as I feel her body squirm under me. I don't need to focus on any other part of her, as I feel the heat in her underwear, as I feel the wetness soak the material around my hand. I pull my hand out just as my wife's eyes open, a perfect moment for her to watch me suck my fingers into my mouth.

"Richard, fuck me." She moans as I pop my fingers out of my mouth.

"I'll do you one better. I'll fuck you until we're making love." I dip down and kiss her hard before I separate us to take her stupid bra thing off of her, so I could stare at her perfect breasts and dark pink nipples. Amelia makes it a point for me to take my shirt and jeans off too, leaving us both with our underwear on. Our tongues intertwine in between every removal of clothing. Amelia feels for my cock over my underwear, and I swear it reminds me of the first time we did this in her room, her childhood room had also been the room where we lost our virginities to each other, and this moment feels just as vulnerable as that one had.

I pull her closer to me, with my hand on the back of her neck, her moaning into the movement and the touch of me. Both of us look at each other as she pumps my cock as it juts out of the underwear's pocket, while I finger her underneath what I now see is her slutty thong. Amelia might've seen my smirk first, or maybe I'd been the one to catch the glint in her eyes, whatever it was, was enough for the both of us to move our underwear to the side just enough for me to slide myself inside her.

"Holy shit." Both of us said in sync.

"You're so fucking tight, Amelia." I had to bite my lip to hold myself back from pushing myself deeper inside her, enjoying her inner walls squeezing my cock.

"I can't remember the last time you've felt this big in me." She says through a moan, as her head falls back onto the bed.

My eyebrow raises, "Really, you can't remember, the last time I had you on this bed, trying to fuck you like a man on a mission?"

Amelia groans as I push myself a little deeper. "Are you insinuating you were a man when you were seventeen?"

The glint in her eyes reappears as she licks her lips, "Do I need to fuck you into remembering how much of a man I was that night?" I growl as I push my cock in even deeper. Amelia winces and moans simultaneously.

"I'm just saying, teenage versions of us are a lot different..." She says as I push the rest of my cock in her. "Oh, god."

"Yeah, I remember you asking for god back then too."

Amelia smiles, "Just shut up and fuck me, Rooster."

I let out another noise that sounds a bit like a growl in answer, as I pull my cock back before thrusting myself back into her. My wife continues to ask for her god as I give her every inch of me.

Chapter
Twenty-Four

Amelia – Present

I couldn't help but smile as Richard brought himself down to nibble on my neck. I didn't think I'd forget what it was like to have my Richard back, my Rooster, but having him on top of me, making love to me, and acting like the man I remembered. It'd been eye-opening, it had been finding ourselves all over again. We had found ourselves in each other, and I never realized it until this moment.

The way Richard looked at me as he fucked me, the look in his eyes as his hands traced down my curvy body, the way his hands held on tight to my stomach and waist as he made love to me. There had been so much I'd never bothered to pay attention to before, like the way his body nearly folded when he realized how broken I actually was. We'd moved past it this far, and I could've given him a million different reasons why we belonged together, but I gave him my truths. I had given him something real, I gave him my heart again. Whether or not

Richard knew it, he'd be the only man to hold my heart, even if he broke it every ten years, I'd give it back to him. I'd never give it back to him if I knew he wouldn't learn from it, but now that I'd known how he felt, how everything had ended up, I was more than sure that Richard Ramsey Greene was the one and only man for me.

Richard gets off of me, and I immediately feel cold, immediately empty without him inside of me. I know he knows, I know he can read the expression on my face, I can do it too after spending half of my life with him, though not nearly as well as Richard can read mine. I start to get up, but he puts one hand between my breasts on my chest to steady me.

"No, no baby. You stay right there." He says with a rasp to his voice, as he lightly pushes me back onto my back. "I never said I was done with you, did I?"

A gasp rises out of me before I'm able to register his tongue on my pussy, licking and sucking. "God, Richard. Don't stop." My hands tangle in his hair as I feel his fingers enter my core as he laps my clit with his tongue. I don't know where my climax ends, but another one builds as his fingers and tongue don't stop. I feel warmth build in me again and again, I've bursted at the seams, and Richard just continues to push me off the edge, for more and more.

"Richard. I. Need. You. In. Me." My words come out with every large gasp of a breath as he doesn't stop.

Richard stops for a moment, looking up at me with a dripping wet chin, "I owe you every orgasm from every moment I've thought about you, every time you were in the other room and I wanted to have you but couldn't."

185

"What? Richard, you can't expect to give me that many in one sitting."

He shakes his head at me, "You're at twelve right now. I think I can at least get to twenty every day. I can't stop yet." Richard dips back down, his tongue taking one slow, languid lick from the spot; his fingers are deep inside me all the way to my clit.

"Richard! It's too much." I pant. "Please." I feel his tongue deepen, with his fingers curling even deeper inside me. I almost scream from the pressure of my orgasm.

"Just a few more, Turtle." Richard mumbles in between his licks. I feel my body tremble through every orgasm, my hips grinding against Richard's stubbly face as I ride his fingers like they're made from the strongest bones I've ever felt. I don't even register when he's slipped his fingers out of me, because he's quickly replaced them with his dick, and I'm moaning at the pressure of his cock entering me. I look up at him like he's been the thing I've been missing in my life for the past year, when he's been right there all along.

"Never let me go, Richard." I say just as I feel the beginning of another orgasm rip through my body, he pumps inside of me slower as he lets me come.

Richard shakes his head, "Never. I'm never going to let you go again. Wherever you are, is where I am." He says as he doesn't stop matching the rhythm of his words. "I'm never letting you go."

I grab onto him, trying to bring him down to me, despite his muscles, he lets me pull him down. I press my lips to his, as I feel him push deeper inside of me, until I hear his groan. My eyes close tight as Richard's lips separate from me, just as I feel as his cum shoots inside of me. His warm cum inside keeps me from making any sudden

186

movements. Richard sighs with his body nearly going limp on top of me, not that I mind. Both of us try to catch our breaths, with him on top of me.

I feel his fingers brush the hair back from my face, when I finally open my eyes to look at Richard. His blue eyes seem lighter now, and he smiles at me like I've just found the answer to his eureka moment. I can't help but smile back when he looks at me like that. I dip my head towards him as his lips meet my forehead.

"You know, you can't just try and run away from me anymore, right?" Richard asks, like he knows my answer already.

"I have nowhere else to run to. You know all of my hiding spots... For now." I answer with a slight smirk on my lips.

"Excuse me?" He says as he pulls himself up to look at me, while also interlacing our hands together and holding me down. "If you run, I better be running next to you with us holding hands."

"Oh, is that right?"

"Do you want me to show you what it would look like if you tried to run from me?"

My brows rise, "Would you have to tie me up?"

"I would. I'd do a lot more than that, though. I'd show you every- thing you'd be missing out on, too." Richard says as he dips to kiss me.

I hum, "Nothing I haven't experienced already." Richard growls, and I chuckle. "I'm kidding, Rooster."

"You better be." He answers with a stern look on his face. I want to laugh, but I give him a quick peck before he grabs my neck and kisses me again, this time with our tongues intertwining. I can just feel his cock pulse still inside of me, wondering if he could actually keep going. I grab onto his muscles and let him pull me as he falls onto the bed

MIKA C.C.

and turn me in the process until I'm on top of him. Our mouths still together, as I feel a small thrust of his hips. I moan into his mouth, how we both still have the stamina to keep going is beyond me, but just as I feel him grow inside of me, a knock comes from my door.

"Who is it?" I yell as Richard growls at me for bothering to respond. I smile at him as he starts by biting my shoulder before kissing up and down my collarbone.

"It's Tanner." The male voice says from the other side of the door.

I'm about to respond to him, but Richard shuts me up with his mouth.

"And Graves." My brother's voice sounds rough from the separation of the rooms.

"." I almost moan, as I try to stop Richard from fucking me with my brother on the other side.

"I'm not done with you." My husband whispers as I feel his arms wrap around me as I try to get off him. I giggle from his fingers, almost tickling me as he squeezes me tight.

"And your parents." My mom shouts. Her voice is what finally snaps Richard's arms to let me go.

"Shit." Both of us say simultaneously as we get off the bed and run for our clothes. I can't help but chuckle when both of us throw our underwear at each other. It feels like we're in a romance book being caught, like teenagers just enjoying each other.

"I can't find my bra," I whisper as I look under the bed.

"You call this a bra?" Richard asks as I push myself up off the floor to see my bra in between his fingers.

"It's technically a bralette." I answer. He hums in response. "What's that supposed to mean?"

"It doesn't do much for them."

I chuckle at his response, "It's just for looks, not support."

He gives me a look as I put the bralette on, and I walk over to him.

"Not you though, you're here for more than just looks and support, aren't you?" I ask, as I grab his chin in my hand.

"Are you comparing your husband to a bra?" He whispers as he pulls me into him. Richard's still missing his shirt as I'm still holding my dress.

"What if I was?" I whisper back as his lips near mine.

"I think you'd have to let me be the only one to hold these." Richard's lips turned up into a slight grin as both of his hands covered my breasts entirely.

"Maybe later, you know when my family isn't in the next room?" I say with a bit of demand in my tone. With that, my husband slowly lets go of my breasts.

Richard groans as he looks around the room, "Fine. Have you seen my shirt?"

"I actually haven't." I take a step back to put my dress on.

"Check the hamper." My mom says from the door. I feel my cheeks heat as I realize she could hear our entire conversation, I cringed thinking of my brother or dad hearing us in here.

Richard opens the hamper and grabs his shirt. I always forgot that the hamper lid had a loose hinge that would snap it closed if a piece of clothing hit the back of the lid just right. He moves out of the way as I go to open the bedroom door and see the entirety of our families standing outside my bedroom door.

"Ramsey Senior, Clara..." I say just as I hear Richard say an expletive as he stumbles just to be right by my side.

189

"Mom? Dad? What are you doing here? I thought you guys were still traveling?" Richard asks with a confused tremble in his voice.

"We didn't hear from you, not that that had been our reason for coming back. But also, Lee and Dianne told us that you two were separated." Richard's mom, Clara explained.

I shot a look at my mom, whose eyes widened as she looked back at me.

"This tells us a different story though." Ramsey Sr. says with his deep voice, as he looks between his son and me.

I look back at Richard and can practically hear his gulp, "Um, yeah, you guys are a little late."

"Does this mean there's no divorce papers?" Clara asks both of us. We both look at each other, remembering what had happened mere hours ago. We could place blame on each other, but we knew neither of us wanted it.

Richard's the first to look back at everyone, he looks ready to cry, and not that it matters who says it, but I put my hand on his chest to stop him.

"We're not getting divorced. We're having a vow renewal."

Richard looks back at me quickly, "What?" As both of our moms gasp and our dads look confused to hell.

"Yep." I say to them before I look back at Richard, "Right on this ranch, in our favorite place."

I watch my husband hold back his tears as his hand wraps around the back of my neck, "That's the dream."

"It is." I say with tears lining my eyes. Richard pulls me in to kiss him deeply but quickly.

"So does that mean I can actually be the officiant this time?" Graves asks as both of us look at our family, I can just see the beginning of a smile on Richard's face from my periphery.

"I don't see why not." My husband answers, and while I could think of plenty of reasons for my brother not to, I just know Graves wouldn't do anything to fuck up my relationship with the man I've been with since I was sixteen.

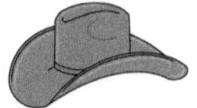

Chapter Twenty-Five

Richard – Past

AMELIA (18), RICHARD (20)

I've been fucking with my tie for twenty minutes. Every time I think it's good, I notice a small imperfection, and my shaky hands immediately go back to fix the tie. I've looked back at the time more than I've needed to, and I'm still actively trying not to worry about where the fuck my best man is. The last time I saw Graves was two nights ago, we'd had our fun playing poker with the entirety of our college baseball team. I look back at myself in the mirror and notice my bow tie slightly off center. My fingers fuck with it again as I hear a bang at the front door. I sigh as I make my way through the Evans family home, it's weird being alone in the house, but the agreement had been made with Graves being here the entire time.

As soon as I open the door, Graves stumbles in, and the sun nearly blinds me from it being low in the sky. With one of my arms outstretched to protect my eyes, I grab for Graves and help him walk further inside, enough for me to shut the door. The smell of hard liquor on his breath immediately lights a fire under my skin. I growl, trying to let out my anger in a positive way that doesn't require me beating the living hell out of him.

"Woohoo! Who's ready for a wedding?!" Graves shouts as he manages to stand tall in a wrinkled suit, with his arms high in the air.

"Not you." I answer, as I grab his arm and pull him into the kitchen.

"Ow. Fuck that hurts." Graves shoves himself off of me, "Why is your hand ten times bigger than my bicep? You're like dinosaur size."

I roll my eyes and blow out a breath, trying to convince myself that he's Amelia's brother. I avoided him for a minute, not giving him any attention after I forced him to sit at the kitchen nook while I fixed him a glass of water. Once I presented him with the glass, Graves looked up at me.

"Is this poison?" He hiccups.

"It's water. Can you drink it? You realize there's a wedding in..." I pause to look at the time on the stove, "Thirty minutes."

"Damn, thirty? That's not long enough for me to fuck the maid of honor!"

"I don't think you want to fuck the maid of honor." I wince as he grabs the glass and chugs it, almost spilling the water on his suit.

"Right, because she's your sister, right? Is she hot?"

I growl, "Graves, I'm being very patient with you, but you do realize my sister is a grown woman with a husband and a child on the way, right?"

My future brother-in-law hums, very similarly to the way Amelia hums.

"You need to get sober for the wedding. Do you think you can take off your jacket? I can probably—" I start as I try to help him take the wrinkled blue jacket off him.

"What? No! You're not controlling me the way you control my sister." Graves swats my hand away as he stands from his seat. "I don't like you, Ramsey. I never did."

I look down and take a deep breath, "You've made that clear."

"I don't understand why you have to be in love with her. Or even why she's in love with you. None of it makes sense. She was meant for the farm, not to follow you around the country for you to play ball."

"Graves..."

"Let me finish!" He shouts as he stumbles as he takes a few steps away from me. "You realize that she's going to lose herself? She's going to be a stepford wife for you, while you're going to go pro, and she's going to hate you. You hear me? She's going to resent you for taking her away from us. From this place. You two might be in love now, but it's not going to last. I bet every last dollar in my pocket right now that it won't." I don't bother looking him in the eyes, as I know Graves never says anything he doesn't mean. I click my tongue after hearing every word he's said and letting it sink in.

I finally look up at him, and have to hold my head high as a sigh, "Well, I'm sorry you feel that way. But there's going to be a wedding anyway, so either you can suck it up and wait for your sister at the altar with me, or you can leave now before the wedding even starts."

Graves puffs out a breath, "I'm doing it for my sister, not for you." I want to growl at him, throw a punch at him, something to get him to understand there's nothing more important than his sister. No matter what Graves says, Amelia will always be my number one.

194

Amelia and I had always talked about having a big wedding, one in a chapel, one with everyone we wanted to share the day with. We had our wedding plans down to a science, but when it came to planning the real wedding, we realized we couldn't afford big, even with her parents footing most of the bill, neither of us wanted to put that on them. We made our ceremony small just so we could have a big party after, that was the one thing we kept big.

After everything Graves had said to me, I still wanted to marry Amelia. I walked through the fields, clearing my head as I headed to the spot where we were going to be married. I walked all the way to that spot where I first met Amelia, the first time she interested me as more than just a friend, the hope she gave me that everyone could be saved in the same way Calliope had been. Just as I reached the stables, white hair fluttered by, a quick neigh was all it took for me to smile. The light trot on the grass had such a hushed tone, excitement shot through me just knowing it had to be Callie walking to me.

"Hey girl." I greeted her as Callie's nose pushed at the side of my head. "Can we leave the hair alone?"

Calliope exhaled hard as I chuckled. I had to push her nose back when I felt her teeth reach for my hair.

"You're very feisty today. You know what's happening, don't you?" I ask as I hold her face, brushing my fingertips lightly through the side of her face. Callie's heavy breath was answered enough. "I'm glad you know me. You probably know me better than my own siblings. You've always got me, Cal. So I bet you can feel how nervous I am right now, huh?" I let out my own deep breath, "I'm gonna take care of her girl. I'm going to make sure she's the happiest she's ever been. I'm not going to let her go, you see that right? Amelia's the one for me, there's no one else like her."

The sound of crunching grass has me stepping away from Calliope as her tail whips. A noise of acknowledgment comes from her as I turn and see my parents walking towards me. My mom with a wide smile on her face with her arm in my father's, his stern look is just another expression we have in common. Seeing them all dressed up on the farm is almost healing. Knowing that my family will become Amelia's, I can feel the love my parents have not just for each other but for Amelia and me, too. My mom comes up to me with her shawl already falling off her shoulders as she gives me a hug. Tears prick my eyes when my dad follows suit and embraces us all together. I never thought it had been possible to have two parents that loved me, especially when they had other kids that were better than me, I couldn't help but be proud of my parents for getting me here. Our embrace ends with a clearing of my dad's throat. It was probably for the best, as I watched my mom wipe away tears when we parted. I couldn't help but wipe her tears, she always cried at weddings, but she'd lost it when my oldest brother got married and then again when my sister got married. This time her tears were silent, almost like she knew this was inevitable for me.

Amelia's parents came out along with the officiant, then Graves and my sister, Mallory. I wanted to focus on how happy Amelia's parents had been for us, but I couldn't help but look at Graves face and the look of disgust he threw my way as he walked with my pregnant sister on his arm. My sister negated his expression with the widest smile I'd ever seen as the two of them walked up to me. Graves immediately avoided a hug and handshake, just standing close by as Mallory wrapped her arms around me in a big hug. Despite her large pregnant belly, her hug was tight and held so much for me.

"You look amazing, Rich." My sister whispered into my ear as I felt her hand pat down my back.

"Thanks, Mal." I said with a squeeze in my hug, hoping it wouldn't pop the baby out. We pulled apart as she looked up at me, like she knew something I didn't.

"You have no idea, do you?"

"No idea about what?" I asked back, with my brows creased. I tried not to pay attention to the way my sister pushed a loose hair of mine back into place.

"You'll see soon enough, big bro." Mallory smiles as she holds my arm for a moment before stepping off to the side.

Our ceremony was a bit unconventional, with only the sounds of the farm leading us to our spots. Our officiant was a deacon from the local church, and the flowers Amelia had wanted were out of season for our early-fall wedding, that seemed to be the only thing that was out of place. But what I forgot was Amelia's dad wasn't where he was supposed to be, missing in action just as a horse neighed. I looked behind me to see Diamond, the black horse with a white diamond shape on her forehead, walk toward us, as we were settled just at the entrance of her shade. Distracted by the horse, I didn't focus ahead of me until my sister's voice calling my name got me to turn back around and find her. Calliope being pulled by Amelia's dad, while Amelia rode in on the horse's back. The white of her dress matched Callie's mane almost perfectly, with just the bottoms of her cowboy boots peeking out of her dress.

Once Calliope had reached me, Amelia's dad had steadied the horse as I walked to her side, Amelia's hand reached out for mine, and I caught her like I always did. I held her as I helped her down.

"God, you're beautiful." Amelia's gaze followed the top of my suit all the way up to my face, until our eyes locked.

"You're not bad yourself, you know?"

"Yeah? So that means you still want to marry me, right?"

"I'm not sure, there seems to be another girl." Amelia answers with a smile as her hands hold onto each side of my bowtie.

I feel my brows crease as I'm ready to question her, but the loud noise of a horse breath attacks my ear. I almost backed away, not realizing Calliope had circled behind me, while I was busy staring at my future wife's beauty.

"Calliope!" Amelia giggles, just about everyone had a chuckle over the horse as Amelia's mom comes to pull Calliope away.

"Can you blame her?" I asked with a smirk.

"It must be the flowers on your suit." Amelia hovers a finger over the baby's breath next to my lapel.

"*Or?*" I ask with a confident brow.

"Or it could very well be my handsome almost husband." She hums as I dip to kiss her lips.

"I like that, *almost* husband."

"We don't have all day," Graves shouts, bursting my bubble with Amelia, as she looks over at her brother, then back at me.

"Let's turn that 'almost' into eternal." Amelia winks at me with her eyes shining brightly in the sun. I look out at the field, at the sun in the sky, waiting for the magic, the one thing this world has always managed to bring us—the perfect weather, the perfect sky on our best days.

My eyes settle back on my almost-wife, as I take her hand in mine and we walk to the officiant. I let every single word that comes from his lips sink in. Loving Amelia has been the easiest thing, but I knew we'd never been through any real problems together. We had forever to go through them, the both of us were just entering our twenties, we'd have a whole lifetime to experience together.

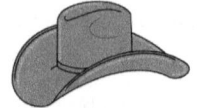

Chapter Twenty-Six

Amelia – Present

"Did you find something blue?" I hear from the door as I lean backwards from the threshold of the bathroom and see Chelsea waving a blue handkerchief.

"Chelsea!" I shout, I don't even put down my eyebrow pencil as I almost run to her, with my hair bobbing in their curlers.

She meets me halfway with a great embrace, she looks amazing in a teal-green dress that falls down to her heels, the dress even has a slit that follows up the side of her thigh.

"Damn, are you trying to look better than me at my vow renewal?"

Chelsea chuckles, flipping her red hair off her shoulder. "No one could possibly take away this day from you. You barely have makeup on, and you look stunning."

"I am in the middle of doing it." I say, holding up my brow wand.

"Ooh. Do you want me to finish it for you? You know how I love to glam my friends up!" She says with a vibrant smile, her purple lipstick making her teeth look even whiter than they already are.

"Sure." I quickly brought her to the bathroom, where I had all my makeup spread out. While she browses through what I have, Chelsea hands me the blue handkerchief, and I inspect it.

"Is everything ready?" She asks while picking up a powder.

"Mostly. I mean, yes, it is. We did our best. I can't believe we've actually figured this out." I say, twiddling with my fingers as Chelsea starts applying makeup to my face.

"Well, of course you two have it figured out. You're you and Ramsey, well, he's Ramsey."

I couldn't help but let out a nervous chuckle, "No, I'm talking about this vow renewal."

"What do you mean?" She sounds concerned when I look in the mirror to see what she's done so far. I let her get back to my face as I answered her.

"I mean, this renewal is pretty much exactly how we wanted our actual wedding to be. We got married right after I turned nineteen and he was freshly twenty-one, so we didn't have any money. He was in college, not playing professionally then. And my parents were—well, they hardly had enough money for me to go to college, so while they were able to pay for the wedding, we couldn't do all the big stuff we wanted."

I pause as Chelsea asks me to close my eyes to apply eyeshadow to my lids.

"Back then it was small, like just our parents and one sibling. So now it's nice to have more than just our family, but our friends too."

"But didn't you guys also get married on the farm? You didn't want to do it inside? This house could easily fit a hundred people." Chelsea says with a chuckle in her voice.

"Yes. We didn't want to change the venue, this place is our history. It's a part of our story. We do plan on having our reception in the house, in case you were wondering."

I hear Chelsea chant the word 'yay' under her breath, and I giggle.

"So now that the day is here and we have everything, and I mean everything we ever wanted for our wedding, I somehow feel like something's missing."

Chelsea makes a noise as I open my eyes to look at her. "Maybe you're just overthinking it?"

"I honestly don't know, maybe I am." I say as we both hear a knock from the front door. Both of us look at the door and then each other. I pull out my phone to check the time. "Weird, it's not even sunset time yet." I walk over and open the door to three girls standing before me, one I've definitely seen before, but the other two I haven't...

"Chelsea asked us to meet her here?" The familiar one says, her eyes pop against the dark blue dress she's wearing.

I turn back to give a look to my redhead friend, she smiles like she knows she just got caught for something that I should forgive her for. Chelsea walks over with arms wide open.

"Madison! Sierra!" Chelsea nearly yells as she gives each of them hugs, then looks at the shorter blonde and sighs, "You must be Nova."

"Yep, that's me." The girl says, she looks young, definitely in her early twenties, if I had to guess. Nova looks right at me, "Can I use your bathroom?"

"Oh, yes. Of course." I open the door even wider to let her in, "Do you guys want to come in?"

"Hey, Amelia, these are the girls I was telling you about. Madison is with Chris, and Sierra here is with the guy in the band."

"Seb isn't really in a band anymore." Sierra says in a monotonous voice.

"Doesn't matter." Chelsea's head shakes with a quick smile. "Richard invited them to the wedding. And I feel like telling you, they've also been through their fair share of their men being absolute assholes. So I was hoping all of you could be friends."

I watch Madison, the girl who looks the most familiar to me, her face contorts like she's uncomfortable. Meanwhile, Sierra looks excited and like she's about to ask me a million questions.

"Oh, this is gonna be so good! Do you have wine?" Sierra asks as she and Chelsea walk into my house. I look back at them for a second before Madison speaks up, as she just barely crosses the threshold.

"Yeah, you know I can't actually drink, right?"

Sierra rolls her eyes, "One drink isn't going to stop that Hayes baby from growing."

"Sierra!" Madison's eyes widen as she looks between me and Chelsea.

"You're pregnant?!" Chelsea shouts as she walks over to Madison. "We've got to celebrate now."

I close the door behind me as Chelsea walks around like she owns the place, and takes the girls to the kitchen just as Nova exits the bathroom. Nova looks at Madison and quickly glues herself to her.

"So you guys must've been friends for a while, right?" I ask as I walk behind Nova.

She looks back at me, and it takes her a moment, but then she smiles, "I was the new member of their cult, but now you're the newest one."

"I don't understand what's going on." I say loud enough for them all to turn to look at me as we exit the hallway into the kitchen.

"We're your bridesmaids, did Richard not tell you this?" Madison asks suddenly.

"That would require my husband talking to me today, and he did not." I gulp, knowing my anxiety is rising with these random women being chosen to walk down with me. I pull out my phone, ready to call him, just as Chelsea swipes the phone from my hands.

"No, no, no. No calling him. You need to get dressed, we'll help with your hair once you're done." Chelsea says as she pockets my phone.

"Chels, c'mon give me my phone back. Richard needs to know this is ridiculous and a bit excessive." With my hand outstretched, Madison high-fives it as if it were meant for a low-five situation.

"So I know we just met, but just get dressed first, and then we can talk about giving you your phone back." Madison smiles tightly. I don't know this woman at all, but her quick response has me walking back to my room to get dressed.

Once I'm done getting on a dress similar but not exact to my old wedding dress, I walk out and the girls all cheer, hollering like it's a dress made for the club, when it's nearly the opposite. I don't bother responding to their noises except to give them a half-hearted smile. Chelsea immediately tends to my hair, releasing all of the curlers. With me in front of Chelsea, Sierra stands close by to help her collect the plastic curlers. Madison and Nova seem to have a quiet conversation about something in the corner, which I don't bother to worry about until Madison walks over to us.

"Are you guys almost done? It's nearly time."

"Time?" I ask as I look for the clock since my phone has been taken hostage, "No, it's not; we still have an hour." The look they all share tells me otherwise.

"Is there something I'm missing?" I ask them, hopeful that one of them will tell me whatever they've been quiet about. They don't say a word. Chelsea brushes out my curls as Sierra helps me into my boots. We're halfway to the door when the doorbell rings.

"There's a doorbell?" Chelsea asks as if she didn't notice the electronic button, "Would've been easier than using the knocker on the door." The girls chuckle as I walk to the door to open it, leaving the rest of them trailing behind me.

My dad smiles as I open it, "You ready for this, baby girl?"

I'm a bit confused, but I nod my head, "It's just a vow renewal, daddy."

He breathes with a chuckle lacing his words, "I'm not sure I'd call it just that." My father offers part of his arm as I take it and walk with him onto the front porch and then down the few sets of stairs. "Your chariot awaits." He says as he walks me around the corner to see a white horse tied to a small tree.

I nearly gasp at how similar this horse looks to Calliope, "What is going on? What is this?"

"Your husband still has a few tricks up his sleeves." My daddy responds, he helps me up on the horse and then removes the tie. I look back at the house to see the girls all walking down holding their long dresses. The wind picks up my hair as the horse trots through the grass, just about halfway to the barn, we wait as the girls make their way ahead of us before we start walking again.

MIKA C.C.

This day feels familiar, the sky in its infinite beauty manages to look like it's on fire with the sunsetting in the sky, with reds, pinks and the higher up I look, even purple. There's three hundred wooden chairs, all filled with people. There's a band playing the song Richard and I first danced to, there are flowers. My bouquet is brought to me as my dad helps me down, an arrangement of baby's breath, sage and lavender. I almost cry because my dad is right, this isn't just a vow renewal. It's the wedding I had dreamed of, the one Richard and I missed out on the first time. I don't even register everyone watching me, not as I'm trying so hard not to cry.

I kept closing my eyes and took multiple deep breaths, to stop myself from crying. It's not enough as there's an actual walkway in between the chairs, the grass is covered with flower petals, and it leads all the way to Richard. I look down at where I'm walking at first, and with my dad holding onto me, it gives me a chance to look everywhere. The people watching us, all of Richard's team and even his siblings are here, not to mention all of my extended family. The band is small and made up of three players just lightly playing, with no vocalist necessary to make the song sound ethereal. Both my mom and Richard's mom are in tears despite them being at our real wedding. By the time I focus on Richard, and really focus on him, I'm in near tears myself. I can't help but be amazed by the man he is, by the only man I've ever loved, the man that's never stopped loving me even when I thought he did.

Richard smiles as I finally make it to him, unsure if I actually walked all those steps to him or floated to him. I swear we're like magnets, always stuck to each other, strong enough to come together even when something gets in our way. Besides Tanner, the rest of the men stand at his side, I barely know, as they're his teammates, smiling towards me.

I try to hold myself together, but just seeing the look in Richard's eyes tells me everything.

"What is happening right now? I thought this was a vow renewal, not this big thing that would make me cry." My shaky voice gives away that I'm about to burst into tears.

"Oh Turtle, this is our wedding." Richard answers while pushing one of my curls behind my ear, "We were just kids when we first got married, we didn't even have a proper reception. This isn't a vow renewal, this is me asking you to marry me right now, to do it in front of everyone we know and love. We're not forgetting our past, we're not going to live like we used to. We're always going to have those memories, that part of us in our hearts—" Richard coughs to clear his throat.

"Richard, what are you saying?" I ask with near tears.

"Marry me again, marry me even though we're already married. I've come too close to losing you, and I've missed spoiling you, and I always planned on giving you everything you've ever wanted. That starts here, with the wedding of your dreams. Would it be so bad to call this our wedding day 2.0?"

"You're ridiculous, you know that, right?"

"Well, at least I didn't stick you with my sisters as your bridesmaids."

I chuckle as I lick my lips, "We're going to talk about that later. Right now, I'm ready to marry my husband again."

Richard's smile widens, "I hoped you'd say that." Seeing him smile with tears just barely falling from his eyes causes a croak to come from me as I feel tears fall from my eyes, he catches them with a finger, "Can't cry for this next part, okay?" He caresses my face with a hand.

"Okay." I answer shakily, as he pulls himself in and plants a small chaste kiss on my lips. "I love you, Rooster."

"I love you, Turtle." Richard says as his hand finds mine and intertwines our fingers. We turn and look at our officiant. My brother...

I've never seen my brother cry, never growing up, not even when he lost his favorite farm animal, but the moment he started to recite the speech meant for me and Richard, was the moment he lost it. I wouldn't call what he did sobbing, but Richard did ask Graves enough times if he was okay. Graves wiped his tears every time, his deep voice didn't match his energy, not until he got to the end that he pulled himself together. We didn't have much else to say besides reciting the words that Graves had us repeat, but before he could start that part, I stopped him.

"If it's okay, I'd like to say something." I said between Graves and Richard, both looked at me a bit shocked and confused by my interruption. Richard's expression looks a bit scared, so I smile to reassure him.

"You've done a lot for me in such a short time, Richard. We've been together for so long, I feel like it's only necessary that I tell you something, give you the words that you need to hear too. It's unfair for me to marry you again without telling you how much I love you. How much you mean to me, how right now I'm having the same butterflies in my stomach that I had the first time I ever kissed you. Our first wedding was so special to me, but I know neither of us expected our future to go the way it did. Now we're older and smarter, and this wedding reminds me so much of what we had wanted back then, a life together, a family and your career in baseball. I can't ask you to retire, it was wrong of me to ask that of you. If you want to stay with your team, you should."

Richard hums, "It's a little late for that, Turtle."

"It's not, I know they're here. I know they'd take you back."

"Amelia, it's okay. It's done. I'd rather never play the game again rather than lose you." He says with his hand tightening around mine, "You are my world, and my world comes first."

"Rooster, please, I'm not just saying this. I mean it. I want you to have your career and me; you shouldn't have to choose between us."

"I'm not choosing between you and the game, I've already made my decision. It's you. It's this place, it's the life I should've chosen from the beginning."

"Are you sure?" I ask, my voice nearly breaking.

"Turtle, you've made me the man I am today. You've helped me get as far as I have in my career, you've made me shine brighter than a trophy. Now it's time for me to get you back to where you shine the brightest."

I look Richard in the eyes, reading the truth in his words and his gaze. I question every part of myself for not realizing how much Richard loves me, but now that I do recognize his love, there's nothing more that I want than to spend every day making it up to him. I want him to realize that I never stopped loving him, that the months we spent apart were spent wishing I was stronger, wishing we'd been able to work through my problems together. I hope Richard sees it all in my eyes the way I can read how much he loves me in his dark blue eyes.

Graves has us finish the last part of his speech, and I put Richard's ring back on his wedding finger. When it's Richard's turn, he pulls out my wedding band. The plain gold band has always been my engagement ring's counterpart, but when he asks me to hold onto it, I go rigid. Confusion trips me up as he pulls out a new band, this one twists like a braid and has diamonds that follow all the way around the band. I think of questioning him, but as I open my mouth, my brother shouts to kiss the bride.

Richard's mouth is on mine, and I lose the reason why I was about to question him. Not as my hands tangle in the back of his hair, as his hands hold me and dip me, I swear we're in a movie with the amount of people cheering us on. I've never heard people clap for a kiss before, and I'm begging for more from Richard. Our kiss deepens as our lips split open and our tongues tangle. I could kiss him like this every day, and I plan to have forever with his lips. When our lips finally part, Richard brings me back upright, and I look as his lips are lined with my lipstick as he smiles.

"I love you so much." we both say at once, I giggle as I watch my husband's smile grow wider. We both turn as my brother announces us as husband and wife, it's surreal as I look out at all of our friends and family and feel the love and happiness from everyone focused on us. The sky is starting to darken with the deep purple with the pink fading over the grass, and I can't help but think that my favorite days will always have a cotton candy sky and my favorite guy at my side.

The End.

Chapter Twenty-Seven

Epilogue

RICHARD - 3 WEEKS LATER

I woke up to a horrible dream, and it wasn't my first since I had married Amelia again, I'd been having this dream that she would be taken away from me. A lot of these dreams were nearing a nightmare, but they never got graphic enough for me to worry. The last one had almost been, I never thought I'd have to be worried about Amelia dying and leaving me, but with everything that had recently happened, maybe it'd been my newfound anxiety of losing the people that meant the most to me.

I got out of bed, careful not to wake my beautiful wife up and dressed in my new typical garb, gray sweatpants and a white undershirt. I barely made it to the truck when I heard the rooster crowing, the sun was barely in the sky, I treaded out to the barn and the chicken's coop, giving them all their breakfast, hoping to shut up the rooster from waking Amelia. The last thing I needed was her waking up earlier than she needed to.

Ever since we married, we'd moved into the ranch house, her brother still lived there too, but his teammates had moved out. I'd been trying to get Graves out of the house, but since he'd rarely been home anymore, I didn't bother to bring it up, at least, until he made his presence known. Now that Amelia and I lived in the house, I didn't have the need to keep the house in Florida. I used the money from selling the house on buying Amelia more farm animals. It started with Clio, the white horse that had looked eerily similar to Callie, that carried Amelia to our wedding, and now our farm included a new rooster and two highland cows. We'd had our hands full, but I still had enough time to go out to the local batting cages in the early morning.

I'd spend maybe two to three days a week waking up before the sun, to head to the cages and get some baseball out of my system. I missed playing centerfield, I missed the game, but hitting the ball had been enough to get it out of my system. I'd always passed an old abandoned baseball field on my way to the batting cages, but as I drove the truck this morning, I noticed a group of young kids playing. I checked the time and date, and noticed the park was still considered closed for another thirty minutes. I told myself I'd just go out there to let them know before heading back to the truck.

I just made it in as one of the kids noticed me and they stopped in the middle of their game. I put my hands up in surrender as if they were going to yell at me for ruining their game.

"Sorry, I don't mean to interrupt your game, but you know the field is considered closed, right?"

"Yeah. So? Are you gonna tell on us?" One of the young boys asked me.

"Jason, shut up!" The boy holding the bat tapped his friend with the tip. "No—I mean, we know it's not, but no one's ever out here, and we're trying to practice before tryouts."

"What school?" I asked with a curious brow.

"The one about ten blocks away." A young female player answered. "The high school doesn't have a field for us to practice in."

"They have a team with tryouts but not a field?"

"The school uses the one at the Y." They answer.

"Ah, I see. Well, don't let me stop you guys from playing, I just wanted to warn you in case you'd get in trouble. I'm new to the area, so I didn't know."

"Thanks." The boy with the bat responded, as the group of the nine of them spread back to their positions. I start to walk away and look back as I watch them play, a couple of them yelling every so often to catch the ball. I barely make it to the truck when I notice Amelia in her pajamas walking towards me.

"Amelia. What are you doing here?"

"You think I don't know where my husband goes almost every day?" She asks, folding her arms over her chest, "I thought you'd be at the cages by now, but I saw the truck and couldn't help but figure out what you were doing here."

"You know that I go to the cages?"

"Please don't insult my intelligence. You honestly thought I wouldn't find out?" Amelia's voice sounds more condescending, and it only makes me feel guilty for a minute.

"I should've known my wife couldn't stay asleep without me being by her side." I tease.

"Sure. It has nothing to do with the rooster calling you out every morning for leaving him."

"I swear I'm going to pluck that chicken and cook him for dinner."

Amelia chuckles, "Like calls to like or something like that."

"Is that from one of those books you read so much?"

"So why are you not coaching them? They look like they need it..." She says with a bemused expression as she looks over at them. I turn to see them struggle at a beginner-level play.

"Since when do you know baseball?" I ask as I look back at her.

"Since I met my husband. Also because one of them just got hit with the ball. Pretty sure that's not supposed to happen."

I chuckled, "You're right about that." Amelia steps closer to me, invading my space and places her hands on my arms.

"Remember how I said you should continue your baseball career?"

"Yeah?"

"Maybe I subconsciously meant you should be teaching, or coaching the game."

"It's such a cliché, though. A major leaguer retiring and coaching."

"Since when are clichés such a bad thing? You and I are considered a cliché too. Are we a bad thing?"

I wrap my arms around her waist, "Never. Nothing about us is a bad thing." I dip my head and kiss her neck.

"Exactly." She hums as my lips trail over her neck more. "Coaching is the next best thing, though." I pull back, ready to question her.

"How so?"

"Well, you'll coach these kids, and who knows, maybe they'll make it to the majors, and you know who they're going to thank for coaching them?"

"Their college coach?"

Amelia smiles, "Maybe, but also the coach that was in the league that actually taught them something."

"Fair enough. Do you even think I'd be a good coach?"

"Yes, without a doubt. You're great with kids. You're like the Gordon Ramsey of baseball, an asshole to adults but a sweetheart to the kids."

"I've never worked with kids before."

"You don't have to if you don't want to. It's just a suggestion."

I look back at the field at the kids playing, "Maybe I should just see how coaching this group goes?"

"Good idea." Amelia answers with a kiss on my cheek. "I'll see you back at home?"

"Of course." I say before I pull her back and give her my lips, I never let us leave the other without giving her my lips on hers. My wife smiles as I watch her back to her car. I turn to the field and head over to the group of teens that desperately need a coach. I clap to get their attention.

"Alright, so which one of you actually watches the major league? Because I can tell you guys right now that you all are missing one key component."

MIKA C.C.

Amelia - One Month Later

I keep looking at Richard, looking at him like he knows my secret. I haven't told a soul yet, it's been too soon to tell anyone. I didn't even want to tell my husband until after the doctor's appointment, but I can't keep it from him. I can't just go to my appointment without him asking, nor can I just say that it's just a quick doctor's visit. There's so much to say and not enough words to say it.

I've been watching my husband act all dutiful and like his life is fulfilled. I know part of him wants to be my horse whisperer, I've seen the way he is with the animals, but I know he wants more even if he hasn't said it. I've been wanting to do more for Richard since the wedding, the feeling that he did so much for me and having done nothing in return for him has made me wish I did more. Richard moved us back to California, he retired from the game and didn't even bat an eyelash.

I'd try for him, help him get back into loving baseball, but maybe this time in a different way.

On top of reopening the farm for summer camp for the kids in the neighborhoods, I decided to surprise Richard with a little token of my gratitude. It hadn't been much, but since the night I caught him watching kids play baseball in the old little league field, it had weighed on me. The spot was less than fifteen minutes from the farmhouse, my parents had asked their agent if the property was for sale, and with a little finessing, I got Richard to co-sign on the *business venture* my parents had needed him for.

Tanner, Luke, and I did the fun stuff. The fun stuff being, cleaning up the field, mowing, repainting the lines and buying a whole new

216

fence and gate so that no critters could get in. That wasn't even the best part, the best had been the addition of the scoreboard and lights, a gift from my parents. Even though they'd helped secure the field, I had paid for it with the money I had saved up.

When it finally came to surprising my husband, I had the sinking feeling he already knew. Between the IVF treatments and working on separate sides of the farm together, I was possibly going to make the man of my dreams' ambition come true. Life had truly thrown us for a loop over the last few years, the last two years more than ever, but now it was our time.

"Remember how I said I don't like being blindfolded outside of the bedroom?" Richard asks from the passenger seat, he blindly tries to reach for me, and I chuckle as his hand hits the center console.

"Hey now, you relax, we're almost there." I grab his hand for reassurance.

"Well, wherever we are, it's not far from the house. So the grocery store?"

"Will you just hush?" It takes me one more turn, and I arrive in the parking lot. Everything is set up perfectly, the banner hanging from the chain link fence has me nervous from the wind, but I have hope that when I undo the tie around his eyes, everything will click for him.

The moment I get out of the car, I grab the fancy helium balloons and tie them up next to the banner. I'm no party planner, but I think what I've done here is the best I could've ever come up with for my husband. After helping Richard out of the truck and onto the sidewalk, I suddenly felt his hands shake. His left hand shakes worse than the right, but the moment I press my lips to his, the shaking stops.

217

"We're here, Rooster." I say just as I take off the blindfold. Richard looks around with an expression of confusion and amazement.

"This is the surprise?" His brows turn in as he scans me and the field before his eyes land on the banner.

"Yep." I respond, staring up at him and the cotton candy sky behind him.

"That banner says my name. Why does that banner say my name?" The confusion in his voice makes me giggle.

"Because we own this field, Richard. Well, you do, mainly."

"What?" I watch as his lips twist upwards.

I smile, "I tricked you when I said my parents had a business venture for you to cosign. You were signing for this field. And for your own little league team."

"You did this? You cleaned it up too?"

"With help from my friends." I answered proudly.

Richard shakes his head, his eyes sparkling, "You amaze me, you know that?" He takes up any space between us, picking me up just to kiss me deeply until I'm weak in the knees. I almost have to catch my breath when he sets me down.

"The blue and pink balloons threw me at first, I thought you were going to tell me something else." Richard says with a sigh, "Could you imagine?" I watch as he scratches his beard.

"We don't have to." I pulled out the test I got from the drugstore just yesterday. I'd been testing myself for two weeks straight just to make sure it was real. The doctor's appointment was set for two days from now, and it seemed like the best time. Richard looks down, almost gasping.

"Wait, what?" He grabs the test from my hand, and I watch him speechless as he looks up from it to look at me, his eyes darting back to the test.

"You're really—?"

I start to sob the moment I watch tears fall from his eyes, "Yes, Rooster. We're getting our baby."

"Fuck yes." He pulls me into him, kissing me until I can't stand anymore, his body lifting me until we're on the hood of the truck, making out like teenagers.

I lose myself with the way I love him. I used to think it was a bad thing, that I was losing a piece of myself, but it's never been that. What I thought I had lost, I had gained, I had lost pieces of myself from my depression, but all of it helped me learn that I had gained empathy and compassion. A love for someone that didn't make it, grief for the loss of my innocence, and yet Richard had pulled me through all of it.

I found myself again in Richard, I found my love for the farm again, my love has always been deep and unconditional. And that's just the beginning, because now I was going to have a baby, our baby, the perfect mixture of Richard and me. Whoever our baby turned out to be, would always be surrounded by love. And I can't wait to tell our baby *our* story and everything that led up to them.

Chapter
Twenty-Eight
Acknowledgements

This is my fourth time writing these and it never gets easier, so I'm just going to say whatever comes out of my noggin.

First of all, I want to say thank you to everyone, everyone that keeps me going. The amount of times I feel imposter syndrome and all of my readers bring me out of it at every book release. So to start, I want to thank my Street Team for y'all being the best and helping me feel better.

I'd also like to say how thankful I am to my family, my husband for always giving me ideas and being my biggest hype person. Add in the fact that he does my covers (last minute) and crushes them every time! My parents are not the inspiration for this book, but they have been together for 33+ years and that just makes me grateful that I've had parents that have stayed together through hard things.

I couldn't have done this without my editor and greatest friend in the world, Amanda, so as usual, the biggest thank you for being my editor, my boss, my PA and as my daughter called you, "stranger partner". You the bestest (don't be editing this part)!

I appreciate my wonderful ARC team. Without you guys to help with the little stuff, especially continuity, I'm not sure I would've made the time to make sure that H&H is cohesive for the entire world to read!

And to all the readers, THANK YOU SO SO MUCH for being my favorite part of all of this. I feel like I repeat myself a lot, but I'm truly grateful and in awe of how many of you stick around and read my stories! I love you all so much! <3

Chapter
Twenty-Nine

About the Author

Mika C.C. is an American writer from Florida. Mika grew up reading and falling in love with fictional worlds, by the time she was ten she was already writing her own stories on her first computer. Mika went to community college and got her Associates degree in Arts with a major in Creative Writing, she went on to further her Creative Writing education at USF. She taught an English class at her local library to young children and continued to write stories on the side. It wasn't until much later, after changing paths to be a Cosmetologist, that she had started her little family. Mika had been a stay at home mom for four years before she realized, writing was her true passion. She's written many stories over the years, some with endings, others she's still working on, but now she has released her first novel to the public. F*ck Happens, a spicy romance novel, as a nod to all of the romance books she's read and to the book community for pushing her to follow her dreams. Just the first of many for Mika...

Find Mika C.C. On Socials!

Instagram.com/author.mika

Tiktok.com/@author.mika

Threads.net/@author.mika

goodreads.com/author_mikacc

facebook.com/author.mikacc

Chapter Thirty

Also by

Mika C.C.

F*ck Happens

Falling For The Angels Series

Coffee & Curveballs

Scoring & Scheming

FIND THEM ALL HERE: https://shorturl.at/jpKY9

www.ingramcontent.com/pod-product-compliance
Lightning Source LLC
Chambersburg PA
CBHW050341030726
47503CB00008B/2557